"Nice car. Maybe someday you could take me for a ride."

Reily fully expected Joe to balk at the idea, just to prove he wasn't at all interested in being anything but her landlord and boss—and even that he did grudgingly.

She was both surprised and a little dismayed when he dug a set of car keys out of his pocket and jingled them.

"But I'm sure you've probably got things to do," she protested.

"What's the matter?" he asked with a look that was pure temptation. "You afraid of a little speed?"

Was he actually *daring* her to go for a ride in his car? A woman who used to ride along for drag races down Hickory Creek road back in Montana?

She propped her hands on her hips. "Honey, your car can't go fast enough to scare me."

The thrill of the challenge was clear in his eyes and the sly grin curling his mouth. "Give me ten minutes to polish it up, and we'll just see about that."

"You're on."

Dear Reader,

I'm so thrilled to be back with the Harlequin Special Edition line. My main focus for the past twenty-four years as a wife, mother and now a grandmother has been my growing family. It's both fun and satisfying to take those experiences and explore them in my stories. The possibilities are endless!

Paradise, Colorado, the setting for this story, is brimming with small-town charm and a bit of quirkiness, and its residents quickly stole my heart. I'm looking forward to visiting them again in future books. Maybe I'll run into you there....

Until then, all the best,

Michelle

NO ORDINARY
JOE

MICHELLE CELMER

Harlequin®

SPECIAL EDITION

Recycling programs
for this product may
not exist in your area.

ISBN-13: 978-0-373-65678-3

NO ORDINARY JOE

MICHELLE CELMER

Bestselling author Michelle Celmer lives in southeastern Michigan with her husband, their three children, two dogs and two cats. When she's not writing or busy being a mom, you can find her in the garden or curled up with a romance novel. And if you twist her arm really hard, you can usually persuade her into a day of power shopping.

Michelle loves to hear from readers. Visit her website, www.michellecelmer.com, or write her at P.O. Box 300, Clawson, MI 48017.

A special thanks to Hillary Scott, Charles Kelly and
Dave Haywood of Lady Antebellum, whose songs,
"Home Is Where the Heart Is" and "Things People Say,"
inspired the idea for this book.

Chapter One

Reily Eckardt sat in the back of the Colorado State Police cruiser, palms sweaty, hands trembling, feeling sick down to her soul with dread. Since she'd left Montana three days ago it had been one disaster after another, but this time she had sunk just about as low as she could go.

First, in her excitement to make good time, she was pulled over for speeding as she crossed the border into Wyoming and had received a costly ticket for her carelessness. Then, halfway across the state, the water pump on her car blew and she'd had to spend the night while the part was ordered and replaced. She'd blown out a tire driving into Colorado, which turned into a four-hour fiasco that put her even further behind schedule and over budget, and she hadn't gotten back on the road until nearly four-thirty in the afternoon. But the icing on her disaster cake hadn't happened until she'd stopped at a gas station just off the highway around eight to grab a cup of coffee. She'd figured she could make up lost time by driving till midnight or so before stopping at a motel for the night. Bad move.

Apparently she'd been more tired than she had realized, or she wouldn't have left her keys in the ignition when she ran inside. And when she'd walked back out, coffee in hand, no car.

The officer who had taken her statement opened the rear door of the cruiser and gestured for her to come out of the air-conditioned interior. She grabbed her purse and climbed out. The sun had dropped below the mountains and a gentle breeze moved the hot, dry air around her. "Did you find it?" she asked, her voice filled with hope and desperation.

He shook his head grimly. "We put an APB out on the plate, but nothing so far."

Her stomach sank a little lower. It had been more than an hour since her car was stolen. Everything she owned in the world, including the money she had saved for the past two years for her new life in Nashville, had been in that car. Her clothes, her photos, her mom's guitar... it was all gone. All that was left of her worldly possessions was her purse and the change from the fifty-dollar bill she'd grabbed from the stash in her suitcase before running inside.

How could she have been so careless?

"What do you think the chances are that it'll turn up?" she asked him.

His grim expression was her answer. "You'll probably want to file a claim with your insurance. Even if it's recovered, I doubt it will be in one piece."

The car was so old, it wasn't insured for theft.

She took a deep breath and steeled herself against the wave of hopelessness and despair, fearing she might be sick right there in the parking lot. Yes, things seemed pretty bad, but life had taught her that they could always get worse. She would get through this and come out swinging. She always did.

She'd already called her cousin in Arkansas and told her she wouldn't be stopping in for a visit. Sweetheart that Luann was, she'd offered Reily a place to crash for a few days. But as a divorcée on welfare with three small children to care for, she didn't have the space or the money to be taking in destitute houseguests. Reily's aunt barely got by on her Social Security so she was in no position to be loaning Reily the money to get to Nashville, and Reily refused to go running back to Montana with her tail between her legs. Besides, she was used to taking care of herself. She would get to Nashville, and she would make it big as a country singer. It just might take a little longer than she anticipated.

"Is there somewhere I can drop you, Miss Eckardt?" the officer asked.

Reily turned to him, really seeing him for the first time. He had a kind face and a paunch belly, and that middle-age softness where there had perhaps once been lean muscle. His name badge said he was Officer Phillip Jeffries, and though he'd probably told her that when he'd arrived on the scene, she had been too shaken to absorb much. Stepping out of the gas station to find the spot where she'd left her car empty had been without a doubt the most surreal experience of her life. Even now it was hard to believe it was really gone. But dwelling on her troubles wouldn't solve them. She needed a plan of action. She took a deep breath and squared her shoulders.

"You could give me a lift to the nearest town," she told Officer Jeffries.

"That would be my hometown of Paradise, about five miles up the road."

It's not as if she had a whole lot of choice. Denver was two hours in the opposite direction. Besides, a small town would be cheaper than a big city. And a town called Paradise, small or not, would have to be pretty nice. "I don't suppose Paradise has a women's shelter or a YWCA?"

"Nope. But we've got the Sunrise Motel if you're looking for cheap. Tell Roberta I sent you and she'll put you up for twenty-five dollars."

It was that or the gas station parking lot. "Sounds good to me."

He let her back into the cruiser—the front passenger seat this time—then climbed into the driver's seat.

"I don't suppose you know if anyone in town is hiring," she asked as he pulled back out onto the interstate.

He glanced over at her. "You planning on sticking around for a while?"

"I don't have a choice. Everything I owned, every penny I've saved, was in that car. I have forty-eight dollars and fifty-two cents to my name. Unless my car is miraculously found, I need to make some money before I can go anywhere."

"You don't have any family who could help you out? Maybe wire you some cash? There's a Western Union at the post office in town."

She shook her head, the knot in her belly cinching tighter. "I'm pretty much on my own."

As a state trooper he probably saw lots of people in bad situations. But that didn't mean he would help her.

"What kind of job would you be looking for?" he asked.

"I can do pretty much anything I set my mind to. But most of my experience is in bartending and waitressing.

And singing. And I have excellent references. You can run a background check or whatever it is that you do. I've never been in trouble with the law. And until two days ago, I never even had a parking ticket."

He glanced her way and said with a grin, "I know."

Of course he would have already checked to see if she had a criminal record or warrants against her.

He was quiet for a minute, then said, "I don't make it a habit of rescuing strangers, but you seem like a nice girl and you're in a pretty bad spot. How about if I take you by Joe's Place? He can usually use an extra hand. And if he can't, the diner at the opposite end of town might have a place for you."

She was so relieved and grateful she could have wept. "You have no idea how much I would appreciate that. I'm so desperate, any job would be a blessing."

"No promises," he said.

"I understand. And thank you, Officer Jeffries."

"Call me P.J.," he said. "Despite thirty years as a state trooper, the folks in Paradise never did take to calling me 'Officer.' I guess that's the problem with small towns."

"I grew up in a small town, too. And I know just what you mean about people not taking you seriously." Since she was ten she had wanted to be a country-western singer, but no one ever believed she would have the guts to go to Nashville. And when she'd finally worked up the courage and saved enough money to start over, even her best friend thought she would come crawling back a failure after a month or two. Which was why she just couldn't go crawling back after only a few days. The town would never let her live it down.

P.J. turned off the highway onto a deserted, two-lane road bordered by farmland on one side and dense wilderness on the other.

"Is Paradise a tourist town?" she asked.

"Nah. We're too far off the highway and too far from any of the good skiing spots. We're mostly a farming community."

It sounded a lot like her hometown in Montana. Which was exactly what she was trying to escape. A cosmic joke perhaps? But it was only temporary, she reminded herself again. She had the feeling she would be doing that a lot until she could get back on the road.

They drove another few miles, before the Sunrise Motel and RV Park came into view up on the left. It was a little run-down from age but it looked clean and well kept. She just hoped it was cheap. They hit a curve in the road, then it dipped and flattened out and Paradise popped up out of the landscape. The welcome sign boasted a population of 1,632.

"This is it," P.J. said, driving past a row of neatly kept little houses and straight down Main Street into downtown, which couldn't have been more than three blocks long. She was no architectural expert, but some of the buildings looked to be over one hundred years old. Like most old towns, some were recently renovated while others sagged in disrepair. But all in all, from what she could see in the waning light, it seemed like a nice little town.

It wasn't Nashville, but it would do until she could make a few dollars and be back on her way.

Lou's Diner occupied the first city block corner and across the road was Parson's General Store. The next corner was home to a feed store and a thrift shop, and across the street were the post office and a dollar store. In between were small shops and professional offices, all closed for the day.

There were a few cars parked in front of the diner, but otherwise the street was deserted until they reached the opposite end of town. Across the street from the VFW hall was Joe's Place, a massive log cabin–style building on the farthest corner of the business district. It was clearly the town hot spot. The street out front and the adjacent parking lot were packed with vehicles. Mostly pickup trucks and a few older-model cars, with a motorcycle or two in the mix.

"This is it," P.J. said.

"It looks busy."

"Joe does a good business. He took it over when his father, Joe Senior, passed three years ago." P.J. pulled up and double-parked near the front door. "Used to be it wasn't much more than the local watering hole, but Joe Junior took the insurance money his daddy left him and gave the place a complete overhaul. Smartest thing he ever did if you ask me."

Country music blasted from inside the bar as P.J. and Reily got out of the cruiser. Butterflies danced in her belly in time with the beat as she followed P.J. to the door. He opened it for her, and what she saw inside took her breath away.

The interior was *gorgeous*. All rich wood and small-town charm. Booths lined both sides of one end of the room and tables filled the space between. The stage and wood-planked dance floor occupied the right side of the opposite end, and on the left wall was a massive and well-stocked bar with an enormous flat-screen television tuned to ESPN. From the walls hung a variety of vintage-looking signs and antique sports equipment and a collection of mounted animal heads. Though dead animals usually creeped her out, somehow it fit.

Joe Junior clearly had spared no expense when he renovated, and if the food was half as appealing as the atmosphere, it was no wonder it was so busy.

P.J. led her across the room to the bar and had her wait while he talked briefly to the bartender, a petite and energetic-looking woman. She gestured him through a door next to the bar. Reily assumed it was probably the kitchen.

She waited, pulse jumping in anticipation, watching as the waitresses hustled food and drink orders to their tables. If it was this busy on a Thursday night, she could only imagine how packed it would be on the weekends. Even if she could only get a position part-time, she could make a killing in tips.

P.J. reappeared a minute later, emerging from the back with a man Reily assumed was the owner.

P.J. gestured her over. "Reily, this is Joe Miller. Joe, this is Reily Eckardt, the woman I told you about."

For some reason she had pictured the owner as older. In his forties or fifties at least. In reality he couldn't have been much older than thirty. He was tall and slender, and attractive in a dark, brooding sort of way. He wore faded blue jeans, a black T-shirt with the bar logo and a deep scowl.

Uh-oh. He did not look happy to have been disturbed.

P.J. took Reily's hand and shook it warmly. "I have to get back on patrol. It was a pleasure to meet you, Miss Eckardt, and I hope everything works out for you. Hopefully I'll be seeing you around. And of course if there's any news about your car I'll call you."

There wouldn't be, and they both knew it. It was long gone.

She smiled anyway and said, "Thank you, Officer."

When he was gone, Joe Miller leaned against the edge of the bar and regarded her with a long, slow, assessing look, his dark eyes lacking even the slightest trace of warmth or friendliness. When he spoke, his voice was so low and deep she had to strain to hear him over the blare of the jukebox. "P.J. tells me you've hit hard times and you're looking for temporary work here in town."

Hard times was an understatement. "I'm pretty desperate, Mr. Miller. If you have any position at all I would be eternally grateful."

"What kind of experience do you have?" he asked.

She had to lean in so close to hear him, she caught the scent of his aftershave. Old Spice, just like her father used to wear. It made him seem slightly less intimidating. "I've waitressed and tended bar for the past six years."

"You've got references?"

"Of course. I *had* a résumé but it was stolen with my car."

He grabbed a pen and an order tablet from behind the bar and handed it to her. "Write down the name and number of your most recent employer."

She hesitated. The bar she'd worked at since she was eighteen was owned by her best friend's father, Abe. Abe was the town gossip. If Joe called him, it would take five minutes flat before the entire city learned that she hadn't made it to Nashville.

But she didn't really have a choice, did she?

She wrote down the name and number and handed it back to him.

"How long were you planning to stay in town?" he asked.

Everything had happened so abruptly, she hadn't had the chance to give it much thought. "I'm not exactly sure."

"I need someone for at least six weeks. If you plan on hanging around for a week or two, then taking off, don't even waste my time."

Yeesh! The guy didn't mince words, did he? "I need enough money for a bus ticket, plus first and last month's rent in a new place once I get to Nashville. So I'm thinking six weeks at least, depending on how many hours you're willing to work me."

His tight-lipped nod said he was satisfied with her answer. He waved over the bartender.

"Lindy, this is Reily. She's going to give you a hand while I make a phone call. Consider this your audition," he told Reily, his expression suggesting that he fully expected her to blow it. Then he slipped through the door to the back. Not the warmest guy in the world, but she was in no position to complain if he was willing to even consider giving her a job. From what she'd seen of the diner, even if they were hiring, the tips would be nothing compared to this place.

Lindy handed Reily an apron. "You don't look familiar. Are you from town?"

Reily secured the apron around her waist. "Just passing through, hoping for temporary work to get me to Tennessee."

"And you chose this hole-in-the-wall town? Why not Denver?"

"I actually hadn't planned to stop at all, but my car was stolen from the gas station off the highway a few miles back. Everything I owned in the world was in it. Including my money."

Lindy gasped and slapped a hand to her chest. "Oh, you poor thing! You lost *everything*?"

"Luckily I had my purse with me so I have my ID and my cell phone, but everything else is gone."

"What about clothes?"

She looked down at the tank top, jeans and cowboy boots she was wearing. "You're lookin' at 'em."

"If you do end up staying in town awhile, I'm sure

we can find someone your size who would be willing to donate some clothes."

"That would be really awesome, because until I can make some money, staying is my only choice."

"Well, I hope it works out here. Since our other bartender, Mark, busted his wrist Monday, it's pretty much been just me and Rick, but he only works a few evenings a week. This weekend is going to be a nightmare, even with Joe behind the bar with me. It's about time he hired me some help."

It sounded as if Joe needed her as badly as she needed him. She mentally crossed her fingers that he would take pity on her.

Lindy pointed out the location of the things she would need, then they got to work taking orders and making drinks, tasks that were second nature to Reily. She chatted up the customers, using a bit of mild flirting when the circumstance necessitated it, finding everyone friendly and curious as to who she was. In the twenty-five or so minutes it took Joe to call on her references, she'd been welcomed to town by at least a dozen people. Paradise sure was a friendly place, and so far it was living up to its name.

Joe reappeared from the back and stepped behind the bar, his expression unreadable. Reily's heart did a quick flip-flop. She hoped he liked what he had heard from Abe.

"So, how did she do?" he asked Lindy.

"She's a natural. And it sounds like she could really use the job." She flashed Reily a grin. "And I'm so desperate for help, she could be the devil incarnate and I would still want you to hire her."

"Well, your references checked out," Joe told Reily. He

added with barely veiled exasperation, "Your old boss is quite the talker, isn't he?"

Knowing Abe, he had probably relayed Reily's entire life story. "Sorry about that. I hope he didn't talk your ear off."

"Close, but he had nothing but praise for your skills, so I guess you're hired."

The stress of the day seemed to drain away and a well of pure relief gushed up inside of her. "Thank you *so* much, Mr. Miller. You have no idea how much I appreciate this."

"It's Joe," he said, but if he felt even a hint of satisfaction for more or less saving her life, it didn't show. "You can start tomorrow. We open for lunch at eleven, but you'll have some paperwork to fill out so be here no later than ten."

"I will."

"We're open Monday through Thursday from eleven to ten, and Friday and Saturday till 2:00 a.m. We're closed Sunday."

"I'm available whenever you need me. The more hours the better."

He nodded sharply, then turned and disappeared back through the door.

"I know what you're probably thinking," Lindy said, and Reily turned to her. "But he's really a great guy once you get to know him."

He could be the biggest jerk on the face of the planet and she wouldn't care, as long as he was a fair and decent employer. Besides, it was temporary.

"Are you and he...together?"

Lindy laughed. "Definitely not. We're just good friends. I've known Joe my whole life. And even if I was interested, he's emotionally unavailable, if you know what I mean."

"I know exactly what you mean." She'd dated a few guys just like him. They weren't worth the heartache they inevitably caused.

She untied her apron and handed it back to Lindy. "Thanks for putting in a good word for me."

"Here," Lindy said, snatching two ten-dollar bills from the tip jar and pressing them into Reily's hand.

"You don't have to do that." Reily tried to give them back, but Lindy shook her head.

"You earned it."

Shelving her pride, she stuffed the bills into her back pocket. "Thank you."

"Tomorrow we'll see about getting you some clothes. I'm guessing you wear a medium in tops and a size five in pants."

"How did you know?"

"I worked in the women's department at the JC Penney in Denver when I was going to college. I know women's fashion. If I ask around, or maybe pull a few strings at the thrift store, I can get you some clothes to hold you over."

"I'm not the type to take a handout, but under the circumstances, I'll take all the help I can get." If the rest of Paradise was even half as nice as Lindy, this temporary detour might not be half-bad. Although she did have reservations about her new boss. She had never worked with anyone so…grumpy. Or maybe she just needed time to get to know him, and vice versa. He was cute enough, not that she was looking to hook up while she was in town. Her only goal was to make the money she needed to get to Nashville. If that meant hanging around this tiny town for six weeks, it was a sacrifice she was more than willing to make.

Chapter Two

Joe sat in a booth across from the bar with a cup of coffee and his laptop, watching his new employee. She sat on a bar stool with her back to him, head bent as she filled out an application and a tax form. Though he wouldn't normally hire a total stranger, especially one just passing through, P.J. seemed to have taken quite a shine to her, and Joe trusted his judgment.

She was dressed in the same clothes as the night before, which he took to mean that she didn't have anything else, and her long, pale blond hair was pulled back in a ponytail that hung halfway down her back and swished when she walked. She was a spunky, high-spirited young woman who had spent most of her life clinging to the short end of a very rickety stick—according to her former employer, that is. He claimed that Reily, who was orphaned as a youngster and raised by an aunt, had been best friends with his daughter since preschool and like a surrogate daughter to him and his wife.

Information Joe really didn't need to know. He didn't care where she came from or how she was raised, as long as she was a hard worker. He wasn't normally in the business of saving people. Not anymore. He'd learned the hard way how futile a venture that could be. It just so happened that she needed a job and he needed a bartender. Simple as that. If she hadn't come along last night, he would have posted a help-wanted sign in the window this morning. It was nothing more than a case of her being in the right place at the right time.

"So who's the girl at the bar?"

He looked up to find Jill, one of his waitresses, standing beside the table. Considering she was usually at least ten minutes late for her shift, he was surprised to see that she'd showed up early.

"Her name is Reily. I hired her last night. She'll be taking over Mark's shift until he's back to work."

Without invitation she slid into the booth. "She doesn't look familiar."

"She's not from around here," he said, and he left it at that. If Reily wanted the other employees to know her life story, she could tell them herself.

"If you were looking for someone, you should have called Ed. He's been out of work since he lost his job at the Dairy Bar."

If her latest loser boyfriend couldn't handle a job scooping chocolate chip mint, he'd never make it in the fast-paced world of bartending. Besides, from what Joe had heard, Ed had lost his job because he was dipping into the register as well as the ice cream. And since it was his bar, and he could hire whoever he pleased, he didn't feel he owed Jill or anyone else an explanation. So he didn't give her one. Instead he turned his attention to the spreadsheet on his screen.

"So, I was thinking of taking Hunter to the lake Sunday, and I thought you and Lily Ann might like to come with us. The kids never get to play together."

That's because Lily Ann was afraid of Jill's six-year-old son. After the one and only playdate she did have with him, she'd come home covered in scrapes and bruises from his overly rough play.

"I have things to do around the house," he told her.

She reached across the table and put her hand over his, giving it a firm squeeze, which quite frankly creeped him out a little. She had a reputation for latching on to any single man willing to tolerate her child. She wasn't unattractive, but she wasn't exactly pretty either, and she had an air of desperation, a neediness that clung to her much like the odor of the cigarettes that she chain-smoked during her break. And though she was a decent waitress, their relationship had never progressed past the bar doors. And never would. Not that she hadn't tried. He didn't doubt that if he asked her out, she would dump loser Ed in seconds flat.

"I know you've had it rough, Joe, but you have to stop sheltering Lily Ann. And you need to get on with your life. That witch you married just isn't worth it."

Teeth gritted, Joe pulled his hand from Jill's clammy grip. That "witch" just happened to be the love of his life. His personal life—and how he chose to raise his daughter—was none of Jill's damned business.

His eyes must have said it all because Jill blinked and jerked her hand back across the table.

"Well, I better get ready," she said with forced cheer, sliding out of the booth. "Let me know if you change your mind about Sunday."

He wouldn't.

At ten-fifteen on the nose, Lindy walked in from the

back. She stepped behind the bar, poured herself a cup of coffee and spoke briefly to Reily. He couldn't hear what was said over the low croon of Randy Travis on the jukebox, but whatever it was evoked a bright smile from Reily. Lindy crossed the bar and slid into the seat across from him.

"Morning, boss. I see your new employee showed up on time."

Her observation surprised him, since she was a die-hard optimist. "Did you think she wouldn't?"

"No, but I think that *you* thought she wouldn't."

He couldn't deny that until she'd walked through the door he hadn't been 100 percent sure Reily would show. In a way he almost wished she hadn't. His life was already complicated enough without adding a needy stranger to the mix.

Lindy grabbed a packet of sugar from the dispenser on the table, tore it open and dumped it in her coffee. "It was a nice thing you did for her."

He winced. "I didn't do it to be nice. You're the one who's been nagging me to hire someone."

"I saw the new schedule in back. You gave her forty hours."

He shrugged. "She's covering Mark's shift."

"Joe, you never start a new employee out at forty hours."

"Her references were good."

She rolled her eyes at him. "Why can't you just admit that you did it to be nice?"

"Because I'm not that nice."

"Then you're really not going to like my next suggestion."

"If I'm not going to like it, why bother telling me?"

She shot him an exasperated look. "She stayed at the Sunrise last night."

He shrugged. "Makes sense. It's close by and it's cheap."

"Well, she can't stay there indefinitely. Not for *six* weeks."

"Why not?"

"For one thing, it's a supreme waste of money, and second, those rooms don't even have a microwave. What she doesn't spend on the room, she'll waste buying meals here or at the diner."

"Why do you care how she spends her money?"

"Because she seems like a nice person and she's in a tough spot."

To hear her old boss tell it, her life had been nothing but one long string of bad luck. Her current situation was no major departure from the norm. "I gave her a job. Isn't that enough?"

"I was thinking, you have that apartment above your garage—"

"Absolutely not." Giving her a job was one thing, but offering her a place to live was out of the question.

"Why not? It's been sitting there empty since—" Lindy caught herself before she actually said the words. She may have been one of his best friends, but there were certain topics of conversation that were off-limits even for her, and that was one of them. "Well, it's been a long time, and Reily could really use a decent place to stay."

"If you're so worried about her, ask her to stay with you."

"In my tiny one-bedroom? Besides, it's not as if I'm asking you to welcome her into your house. And if you take a minute to consider it, I think you'll agree that it's the charitable thing to do."

That didn't mean it was smart.

"You haven't known her long enough to dislike her, so I can only assume that her looks are the issue here."

"Her looks?"

"You may live like a monk, but you aren't one. I'm sure you've noticed that Reily is very pretty."

Of course he had. He may have been celibate for the last two years, but he wasn't *dead*. Although sometimes it felt that way. But he'd noticed Reily the minute he saw her standing by the bar last night, looking shell-shocked and desperate. Something deep inside of him had stirred. An itchy, restless sort of feeling that he hadn't experienced in a very long time. Until then he'd nearly forgotten what it felt like to be attracted to another human being. He thought that part of him had died, but apparently it had only been sleeping.

All the more reason to stay the hell away from her.

"She's not my type," he told Lindy.

She smiled. "Then letting her stay in the apartment shouldn't be a problem."

The really sad thing was that two years ago he wouldn't have hesitated to offer her the space. He would have *wanted* to help her, because that was the sort of person he'd been. It was a stark reminder of how much things had changed since then. There were times when he would do anything to be that man again, but it was a risk he just couldn't take. For Lily Ann's sake he had to keep his head on straight. They had both been hurt enough.

But by helping Reily, wouldn't he be setting a good example for his daughter? Besides, he could see that Lindy wasn't going to let up. She would nag him until he caved.

He mumbled a curse and shook his head. "I suppose you expect me to let her stay there for free."

"Not at all. Besides, I think she's the type of person who would insist on paying some sort of reasonable rent."

She was probably right. Desperate as Reily was, she didn't strike Joe as someone who would accept a handout. Not if what her old boss had said was true. He had told Joe that she was one of the hardest working, most responsible young women he knew.

"Hypothetically speaking, what would you consider reasonable rent?" he asked Lindy, not that he'd make his mind up about anything just yet. "The last tenant paid eighty a week, but that was a long time ago."

"Maybe…sixty dollars a week."

His brows rose.

"It's not like you're hurting for money, and it sounds as if she could really use a break."

She was right about the money. Renting the space had been convenient during the bar renovations when his income was nonexistent, but now business was booming. Sixty a week would more than cover the utilities.

He nearly groaned out loud. He couldn't believe he was actually considering this. But he had the means to help Reily, so wasn't it his obligation as a decent human being?

His father would have thought so. Hell, he probably would have insisted he give it to her free of charge. He would have insisted.

Reily hopped down from the bar stool and, ponytail swishing, crossed the room to where he and Lindy sat. "Finished," she said, handing him the forms.

Lindy grabbed her coffee and slid out of the booth. "Well, I'm sure you have things to discuss," she said, shooting Joe a meaningful look. Then she told Reily, "When you're finished we'll start your training."

Reily sat in the seat Lindy vacated and waited while

Joe looked over her application. She'd listed a high school diploma as her highest level of education, which was about what he'd expected considering her circumstances. Had it not been for the small trust his maternal grandparents had left for him, he wouldn't have been able to afford college either. The money hadn't done much to anesthetize the sting of his mother's abandonment, but it probably went a long way toward easing their guilty consciences.

"Everything seems to be in order," he said, setting the papers beside his computer.

"So, I'm curious as to what Abe told you about me," she said, watching him with wary blue eyes.

"I get the impression that there wasn't much he didn't tell me."

She sighed. "That's sort of what I figured. He's something of a gossip."

"If it's any consolation, he seems to really care about you."

"I know he does. He and his wife have been like surrogate parents since my mom and dad died."

"Why don't you ask them for help?" he said, realizing immediately that it was none of his damned business. He didn't need or want to know any more about her life than was necessary.

"I have to do this on my own," she said. She hesitated a second, then asked, "You didn't happen to mention *why* I needed a job, did you?"

"I pretty much just listened. And when he commented on the weather down here in Nashville, I didn't correct him."

Her relief was clear on her face. "I appreciate that. I'd just as soon let everyone believe I made it to Tennessee."

"The way he talked, he seemed to think you would be back in Montana soon."

"Yeah, that's the general consensus in my hometown. They all think I'm going to come crawling back a failure." She jutted out her chin and flashed a look that was 110 percent stubborn. "I intend to prove them all wrong."

Abe had never mentioned why she was bound for Nashville, but Joe assumed it had something to do with the music business. In which case the odds weren't exactly in her favor.

"Lindy mentioned that you're staying at the Sunrise," he said.

"There don't seem to be many other options."

Only one, though he still wasn't convinced it was a good idea. "I've got a small apartment above my garage. It's not much, but it's furnished and it has a small kitchen. And it's only a few blocks from here. You can use it if you want to."

"How much?"

"Sixty a week."

"That's pretty cheap," she said. Instead of looking grateful for the offer, she frowned and chewed her lower lip.

So much for trying to help out a stranger in need, he thought, feeling slighted. Which was ridiculous since he hadn't even wanted her there in the first place. "I could charge more."

She eyed him with suspicion. "I'm just wondering, what's the catch?"

"There's no *catch*. Lindy thought you might want to stay there."

She brightened a little. "Oh, it was Lindy's idea?"

Did she think he was incapable of doing something nice? And why did he even care what she thought? "What difference does it make whose idea it was?" he snapped, sounding harsher than he'd intended. "Do you want it or not?"

His tone didn't seem to faze her. She leaned forward in her seat and met his gaze squarely. "Put yourself in my position, Joe. You're a single girl in a strange city with twenty bucks to your name, and some man you've known all of about twenty minutes offers to put you up for practically nothing in his swanky garage apartment. Can you honestly say you wouldn't be just a little wary?"

When she said it like that, it did sound a little suspicious. And though the apartment was far from *swanky,* he could see her point. She was a young, attractive woman stuck in an unfamiliar place, dependent on the charity of a bunch of strangers to survive. That had to be scary as hell, even though her demeanor would suggest the opposite.

It made him think of Beth, and how many nights he lay awake, wondering if she was okay, if she'd found a decent place to live, friends she could trust. He could only hope that she had been as cautious then as Reily was now.

She had every right to question his motives. Not just the right, but the *obligation.* And for her trouble, he was acting like a coldhearted jerk.

Was he really so jaded? So insensitive?

Maybe Lindy was right. Maybe his attitude was a defense mechanism, because he would have to be blind not to notice how attractive she was. It wasn't her fault that he had lousy luck with women.

"I see your point," he told her.

"That's why I felt better knowing it was Lindy's idea. I didn't mean it as an insult or a slight. I really do appreciate the offer."

"I guess I hadn't considered the full implications of

your situation. I don't blame you for being cautious. For what it's worth, there's a chain lock on the apartment door and my aunt Sue lives in the house right next door. I can give her the spare key to hold on to if it makes you feel more comfortable. And anyone in town will vouch for my character. But if you don't want to stay there, I won't hold it against you."

"Could I have the day to think about it?"

"Of course." Maybe there was a little bit of the old Joe still left in there somewhere, because he found himself actually wanting to help her, the way he hoped someone would have done for Beth. "Take all the time you need."

"Thanks." She smiled at him, her gaze settling on his face, then her eyes caught and locked on his, and his heart actually skipped a beat. Beneath the uncompromising defiance and strength of will was a vulnerability and apprehension that yanked at his heartstrings. She wasn't nearly as tough as she wanted everyone to think, and he felt the strangest urge to pull her into his arms and hold her. To smooth back the long, silky strands of her pale hair brushing her cheeks and tell her not to worry, that everything would be okay.

Hard as he tried to look away, her blue gaze captivated him. It was she who finally lowered her eyes and broke the spell.

"Well," she said after a brief, awkward silence. "I guess I should get to my training."

She slid out of the booth and he found himself following her with his eyes as she crossed to the bar, admiring the way her behind swayed beneath a snug pair of faded skinny jeans. She wasn't voluptuous by any means, but she wasn't Hollywood-thin either. She had just the right amount of curves for her height. For the briefest of instants he let himself imagine what it would be like to touch her, to tangle his fingers in the long, silky mane that hung down her back. To brush his lips over hers…

He realized he was actually getting aroused and peeled his eyes away.

His libido had been safely compartmentalized and locked away for the better part of two years. In all that time he hadn't felt so much as a twinge of attraction to any woman, yet here he was reeling from a full-blown case of pulse-pounding lust for a virtual stranger. There had to be something seriously wrong with him.

He had the sinking feeling that for the next six weeks, this woman was going to be nothing but trouble.

Chapter Three

Reily stepped behind the bar, poured herself a tall glass of ice-cold water and guzzled it in the vain attempt to douse the flames burning up her insides. The look Joe had given her had been so jam-packed with raw need and pent-up sexual desire, it's a wonder her panties hadn't burst into flames. For an emotionally unavailable guy, he wasn't doing a very good job of hiding his feelings. Honestly, she liked it better when Joe regarded her as an unfortunate inconvenience. She had a defense for that. But the feelings she was having now…holy cow.

She had dated quite a few men, and even felt strong sexual attraction to a couple of them, but never quite like this. Not this heart-pounding, grab-his-shirt-and-haul-him-across-the-table-for-a-kiss *lust*. And he wasn't even her type! She preferred men who were easygoing and fun-loving. Someone she could laugh with. Joe didn't even seem to have the capacity to *smile*.

She refilled her glass and took another swallow, when what she should have done was dump the darned thing over her head. Was it possible that she had just gotten her first glimpse of the real Joe? Beneath the dark and brooding exterior, was there a warm, sensitive and sexy man? And suppose there was? What then? She was leaving in six weeks. The last thing she had time for was a complicated emotional attachment.

Lindy emerged from the back and joined her behind the bar. "So, are you ready to…" She trailed off, a frown furrowing her brow when her eyes settled on Reily. "Hey, are you all right?"

"Of course," she said, dumping the rest of the water in the sink and setting her glass in the dirty-dish tub. "Why wouldn't I be?"

"Your cheeks are red as apples."

She reached up to press her palm to her face. Her cheek was furnace-hot. "I guess I'm a little overheated."

"Do you feel sick, like you might have a fever?"

She felt feverish all right, but not the kind caused by a virus. "I think it's just been a crazy couple of days, and it's starting to catch up with me."

After what she'd been through, who wouldn't feel a little discombobulated? Maybe this irrational attraction to Joe was just a reaction to the stress of what had been a highly emotional situation.

Lindy clucked sympathetically. "You poor thing. Well, if it helps at all I just got off the phone with my friend Zoey. She's your size and she has a couple of garbage bags full of clothes she was planning to give to the thrift store. She's going to give them to you instead. She said she'll drop them by the bar later this afternoon. Zoey's dad is not only the mayor, but the most successful businessman in town, and he tends to spoil her. She prides herself on always looking her best, and she gets a whole new wardrobe every season, so I'm sure there'll be some really good stuff in there."

"I don't even know how to thank you."

Lindy shrugged like it was no big deal. "I believe in karma. What goes around comes around."

If that was true, then something really awesome was bound to happen to Lindy. "Joe said that you suggested I stay in his garage apartment."

"It would be way better than living at the Sunrise for six weeks. And a lot cheaper." She handed Reily an apron and tied hers around her waist. "Are you going to stay there?"

"I'm not sure."

Lindy looked surprised. "Why not?"

"If you were in a strange town where you didn't know a soul, would you stay in the garage apartment of some man you'd just met?"

Lindy frowned. "Oh. I guess I hadn't looked at it that way. For what it's worth, I've known Joe my entire life. He's one of my best friends. He may be a little cranky at times, but he's about as noble and trustworthy as they come. He wouldn't hurt a flea. And there isn't a man or woman in all of Paradise who will tell you any different."

She knew she should seriously consider it, but after what had just happened in the booth, maybe it wouldn't be such a great idea. Not that she'd felt threatened or violated. Quite the opposite. Which was why she couldn't help thinking it would be best to stay as far away from Joe as possible. On the other hand, the more money she made, the sooner she could be on her way to Tennessee. Six weeks wasn't much time to save what she needed. Cheap rent could be her ticket out of here.

Besides, as the day progressed and the lunch rush hit,

she began to realize that seeing a lot of Joe might not be a problem. He seemed to spend most of his time in the back, either in the kitchen or his office. And when he was around, he more or less ignored her. He was so clearly not interested in her, she began to wonder if what had happened in the booth earlier had been a figment of her imagination.

By two o'clock, when the lunch rush had officially ended, Reily had made up her mind about Joe's offer. She left Lindy to serve the handful of regulars sitting at the bar watching the wide-screen and went into the back to talk to Joe. He was in his office working at the computer. When she rapped on the door, he motioned her inside.

"Have you got a second?" she asked.

He pushed back from his desk, folding his arms over his chest, looking mildly put out.

"I've been thinking about it, and if the offer is still good, I'd like to rent your apartment."

He nodded. "Okay."

"If you'd like me to sign a lease—"

"That won't be necessary."

She pulled out the cash she had left after paying for the room last night and the essentials she'd picked up at Parson's General Store on her way in to work. "I can give you the rest after we split up the tips for the lunch shift."

He looked at the cash, then at her. "Is that all the money you have?"

"It's fine. I can live off tips until I get my first check."

He mumbled something under his breath, then said in a voice laced with irritation, "Keep it."

"But—"

"I'm not leaving you with no cash," he snapped. "I'll take the rent out of your first check."

The guy did nice things, he just did them so...grudgingly. Which left her wondering where the understanding, semi-compassionate man from earlier that day had disappeared to. Maybe she had only been seeing what she wanted to see. "Are you sure?"

"I'm sure."

"In that case, thank you."

Lindy stepped into Joe's office with two stuffed black trash bags. "Hey, Reily, Zoey just dropped these by."

She took the bags from Lindy. They were heavy. "Is she still here?"

"She had to get back to work. She said she'll try to stop in later tonight. But don't worry, I thanked her for you."

Reily had been hoping to meet her, and of course she wanted to thank her personally. Although odds were, in a town this size, she would run into her at some point in the next six weeks.

When Lindy left, Joe looked from the bags to Reily, clearly curious as to what they contained.

"They're full of clothes," Reily told him. "Everything I owned was stolen with my car, so Lindy's friend Zoey dropped some hand-me-downs off for me. Would you mind if I keep these in your office until I'm off tonight? They won't fit in my locker."

"I have to run home for a few minutes," Joe said. "Why don't you come with me and we can get you settled in. Unless you feel you need more time to train before the dinner rush."

"Not really." After eight years, bartending was pretty much second nature. "I'll go tell Lindy I'm leaving."

He pushed himself up from his chair and walked around the desk, nodding to the bags she was still clutching. "I'll take those."

"That's okay, I can—"

He pinned her with a look that said it would be in her best interest not to argue. A sort of, *let me be nice or else.*

Okay. She held the bags up for him to take.

"My truck is parked out back."

Which she took to mean, as he headed for the back door, that he wanted her to meet him out there. Because apparently it would kill him to actually say the words.

Shaking her head with exasperation, she hurried out to the bar and told Lindy she was leaving for a bit.

"Things won't pick back up until at least four-thirty, so take some time to get settled in," Lindy told her. Then she handed her a thick fold of bills. "Lunch tips."

She stuffed them into the pocket of her jeans. "Thanks. This will definitely come in handy."

Reily went into the back, grabbed her purse and purchases from her locker and said goodbye to the day cooks, Ray and Al, as she walked through the kitchen to the back door and pushed out into the afternoon sunshine.

Jill, one of the waitresses, stood just outside the door smoking a cigarette. She and Reily hadn't had much time to get acquainted, but she seemed nice enough.

"Shift over already?" she asked Reily, taking a long, deep drag and exhaling a cloud of smoke into the hot, dry air.

"I'm taking off for a couple of hours, but I'll be back."

She eyed Reily suspiciously. "Does Joe know that you're leaving?"

The words had barely left her mouth when Joe pulled up beside them in a newer-model, dark blue pickup.

"He knows," Reily told her. "See you later."

Jill's openmouthed look of disbelief was the last thing she saw as she climbed in and buckled her seat belt. Though why Jill would care if Reily left with Joe, she didn't have a clue.

Without so much as a glance Reily's way, Joe put the truck into gear and pulled out of the lot. He headed down Main Street into town, which was bustling with cars and people, and turned left at Third Street, taking them into a residential section. Most of the homes were older but well tended and charming, with postage-stamp lots and tidy lawns. Not unlike the neighborhood she'd lived in before her parents had died, before she'd moved into the shabby little one-bedroom trailer with her aunt. Reily hadn't even had her own bedroom, just a corner in the living room to keep her things and a foldout sofa to sleep on.

Joe drove two blocks down, then took a right at High Street. The lots were much larger and the houses sparser. Near the end of the block he turned into the driveway of a white-picket-fenced, craftsman-style home with deep green siding and a wide front porch flanked by white ta-pered pillars. It was as warm and charming as a Norman Rockwell painting, and not at all what she would have expected from a single guy.

He pulled up the driveway and parked in front of a double-car, two-story garage. The first thing Reily no-ticed as she opened the door and climbed out was the pur-ple little-girl's bike leaning against the side of the garage. In the backyard, which had to be at least two hundred feet wide and twice that in length, she could see a swing set and a playhouse that looked like a scaled-down and simplified version of the main house. There was also a sandbox, a red Radio Flyer wagon and various other toys scattered across the lawn.

Did Joe have *kids?*

As if on cue, the side door flew open and a little girl shot out onto the driveway in a blur of fine, curly blond hair, pink shorts, white tank top and purple flip-flops.

"Daddy!" she shrieked, vaulting herself into his out-stretched arms. "It came out! It came out!"

She opened her mouth wide, showing off a missing front tooth. Joe smiled at his daughter—a real, honest-to-goodness smile—and the effect was utterly devastating. He was handsome enough when he was all dark and gloomy, but when he showed some teeth? Good Lord, she practically had to fan her face.

Lindy hadn't mentioned Joe ever being married. Not that it mattered either way to Reily. It was just hard to imagine him ever having the kind of optimism it took to step up to the altar.

"Did you give it to Aunt Sue to put under your pillow tonight?" Joe asked. She nodded enthusiastically, then she noticed Reily standing there watching them.

Her brow dipped in a look that was 100 percent Joe, and she demanded, "Who are you?"

Not shy, was she?

"Lily Ann, where are your manners?" he scolded. "This is Miss Eckardt. She works at the bar and she's going to stay in the garage apartment for a while."

"It's nice to meet you, Lily Ann," Reily said. "How old are you?"

"Five," Lily Ann said, holding up the digits of her left hand. "Your hair is pretty. I want long hair, too, but Daddy says it gets too tangly because it's curly."

"And I've always wanted curly hair," Reily said with a smile. "Mine is so straight and boring."

Joe gave his daughter a kiss on the cheek and set her back down on the driveway, giving her bottom a firm pat. "Go on back inside. I'll be in as soon as I show Miss Eckardt the apartment."

She scurried for the door and disappeared inside the house.

"She's adorable," Reily said as the screen door slammed shut with a sharp bang.

"And don't think she doesn't know it." He grabbed her bags from the bed of the truck, then gestured to a set of wood stairs that hugged the side of the garage. "It's this way."

She followed him up the narrow staircase, trying hard to ignore the fact that he had a really cute behind. Not only was he brooding and pessimistic, but he had an adorable daughter to boot. The situation had *complicated* written all over it.

He paused on the small landing at the top, pulled his keys from his jeans pocket and unlocked the door. A wave of stale, hot air rushed out as he pulled it open. He dropped her bags inside and walked straight over to a window that overlooked the backyard. He pushed back the curtains and lifted the sash, letting sunshine and a rush of fresh air into the room. The living space was cozy and welcoming, with two mismatched, floral-print, hand-me-down chairs; a scarred wood coffee table; and a matching pair of brass floor lamps. The kitchenette was small and basic, but functional, with a two-burner stove and an economy-size refrigerator.

"This is nice," she said.

"There's a window air conditioner in the bedroom to keep you cool at night," he said. "And there're fresh linens and towels in the dresser drawer."

She crossed the room and peeked into the bedroom. It was barely large enough to hold a full-size bed and small chest of drawers. The bathroom was nothing more than a sink, toilet and cramped shower stall, but it was clean. It beat the hell out of staying at the Sunrise for six weeks.

"The key is on a hook in the kitchen cupboard," Joe said, and she turned to him. He stood by the door, arms folded, expression dark. "If you want, I can give Aunt Sue my master key to hold on to."

"That won't be necessary." He may have been a little cranky, but she didn't think he was dangerous. Especially now that she knew he had a daughter, although she wasn't sure why that would make a difference.

"So, it's just you and your daughter?" she asked him.

"Yep."

"Lily Ann's mommy—"

"Isn't around," he said. And he clearly did not want to talk about it. Not with her anyway. "I'll be heading back to the bar in half an hour if you want a ride."

"I think I'll walk." Now that she had a little extra money, she could splurge and maybe find a cheap blow-dryer and curling iron at the thrift store.

Joe shrugged. "Suit yourself."

"Thanks for offering. And just so you know, I don't expect rides to and from work to be part of the deal."

"Good, because they're not." He turned toward the door and started out, then hesitated, turned back to Reily and said, "She left us two years ago."

It took a second to realize that he was talking about Lily Ann's mommy. He may as well have been talking about the weather for all the emotion he showed, but that probably only meant he didn't want her to know how deeply he'd been hurt. It sure explained why he would be emotionally unavailable.

She wasn't sure how to respond, but it didn't matter because he never gave her the chance. He turned and walked out, shutting the door firmly behind him. She listened to the thump of his footsteps as he descended the stairs, wondering what had happened between him and Lily Ann's mother that would make her leave. What would possess a woman to leave her own child?

Why did she even care? She had her own problems to figure out. She barely knew the guy. Considering this weird little fascination she seemed to have with him, it would be in her best interest to keep it that way.

Joe headed to the side door, wondering why he'd felt compelled to tell Reily about his ex-wife. His life was none of her business. But she was bound to hear about it from someone eventually, so why not him? That was the problem with small towns. Everybody was always in everyone else's business. When Beth left, the dust had barely settled from her tires before everyone knew.

He pulled open the side door and stepped into the kitchen. Aunt Sue stood at the stove, stirring the contents of a soup pot. She looked over at him and smiled. "I guess Lily Ann told you about her tooth."

"The second I pulled up," he said, giving her a kiss on the cheek.

"I put it in an envelope on her dresser so she wouldn't lose it."

He leaned in to peek at whatever she was cooking.

"White chicken chili," she said.

One of his all-time favorites. "Smells delicious."

"Lily Ann said something about you showing the apartment. I didn't realize that you'd decided to rent it out again."

He grabbed a wedge of corn bread from a plate on the kitchen table and took a bite, crumbs falling on the front of his T-shirt. "I didn't."

She turned to him, wiping her hands on the apron tied around her ample waist. "Would this have something to do with the young woman you hired?"

He shook his head. "Word sure does get around fast, doesn't it?"

"Phyllis and Buster had lunch at the bar today, and of course she had to call me and find out who she is. I take it she's not from around here."

"Her name is Reily Eckardt. She's passing through on her way to Tennessee." He relayed the story P.J. had told him when he'd brought Reily in the night before.

"Oh, good Lord!" Aunt Sue slapped a hand over her bosom. "That poor girl. It was sweet of you to help her out."

Her words grated at him. "I didn't do it to be nice. I needed a bartender, and it was Lindy's idea to let her stay in the apartment."

She pinned him with her trademark stern look. "Would it kill you to admit that you're a compassionate and caring person?"

"I'm not." *Not anymore.*

"Well, there's a little girl in there with her butt parked in front of the television who sure thinks you are."

And he couldn't imagine what his life would be like without her. He walked over to the kitchen doorway to peer into the front room. His little girl sat cross-legged in front of the television, mesmerized by cartoons. The love he felt for her was so intense and all-encompassing it almost hurt to breathe. Having Lily Ann had given him the will to keep going when Beth left. Everything he did was for his daughter, to ensure that she grew up healthy and happy and always knowing that she was loved. Despite her mother. Because when it came to being abandoned, he knew just how it felt. His own mother hadn't stuck around to see his first birthday.

"So how long is this Reily planning to stay?" Aunt Sue asked.

"Six weeks, until Mark is back to work." Too long as far as he was concerned. After that sexually charged moment in the booth this morning, he'd spent the following few hours in his office getting next to nothing done thanks to the random, impure thoughts he couldn't seem to shake. He'd begun to seriously regret offering her the apartment in the first place, and had held out some hope that she would turn him down. No such luck, of course. That's what he got for trying to be a nice guy. It always had a way of blowing up in his face.

"In that case, I should probably put together a housewarming basket. It sounds as if she could use a few things."

He turned back to his aunt and shrugged. "Suit yourself."

"Phyllis mentioned that Reily is quite a looker," she said with that mischievous glint in her eye that he knew all too well. "Cute as a button, I think were her exact words."

"I hadn't noticed," he said, feigning disinterest. She wasn't buying it.

"It's been two years, Joey. Don't you think it's about time you got on with your life?"

"That's exactly what I'm doing. I have a daughter to care for and a bar to run."

She propped her hands on her hips. "You know what I mean."

He did, but his love life, or lack of one, was nobody else's business. "I don't have time for a relationship. Especially with a virtual stranger."

"If you got to know her she wouldn't be a stranger, now would she? Besides, it doesn't have to be her. There are plenty of other eligible women in town. You've been out of the pool for so long, would it hurt to get your feet a little wet?"

Past experience had taught him that he wasn't much of a swimmer. Knowing his luck, he would slip on the edge, fall into the deep end and get sucked under.

Chapter Four

Lindy's friend Zoey had awesome taste in clothes. Reily dumped both bags out onto the bed to sort them. Other than undergarments, she wouldn't have to buy a single stitch of clothing. There were jeans and shorts and shirts, blouses, T-shirts and tank tops. There were even two bikini bathing suits and a couple of luxuriously soft satin nightshirts. Everything looked brand-new, or close to it, and had been freshly laundered.

As she neatly folded and tucked everything into the dresser drawers, singing to herself to keep her vocal cords conditioned, she heard the engine of Joe's truck roar to life. She glanced out the side window just in time to see him slowly backing out of the driveway. He wasn't gone two minutes when she heard a noise behind her and whipped around to find Lily Ann standing in the bedroom doorway. "Well, hi there."

"That song was pretty."

Reily smiled. "Oh, thank you. My mommy used to sing that to me."

Lily Ann nodded at the bed and said matter-of-factly, "Mr. Pete keeps his clothes in a black garbage bag too. And he sleeps in the park, because Aunt Sue says he gots a couple of screws loose. But I like him 'cause he makes funny faces and talks to himself."

The little girl had just compared her to a mentally challenged homeless person. Swell. But she didn't bother trying to explain why her clothes had been in garbage bags.

"Honey, are you supposed to be here?" Reily asked. She was willing to bet Joe wouldn't appreciate his daughter hanging around with a total stranger.

She got her answer when a female voice called firmly from outside, "Lily Ann Miller, are you up there?"

Her lower lip lodged guiltily between her teeth, Lily Ann spun around and scurried for the door. Reily heard the slap of her rubber flip-flops as she charged down the stairs.

Reily walked to the door and looked out to the ground below. At the base of the stairs stood a portly woman of about sixty. Her salt-and-pepper hair was twisted into a loose bun at the back of her head, and she wore a sundress and rubber flip-flops. She was as short as she was wide, with a warm, friendly smile.

"You must be Reily," she called, shading the sun from her eyes with one pudgy hand. "I'm Sue. Sorry if Lily Ann was bothering you."

"She wasn't," Reily assured her.

"It must be hot as blazes up there. Why don't you come down for a cold glass of lemonade?"

It was hot, and though Reily had hoped to stop at the thrift store on her way back to work, a cold glass of lemonade did sound refreshing. And of course she wanted to get to know her new neighbor, and maybe learn a little more about her boss/landlord. The shopping could wait until her break tomorrow.

"I'd love one," she told Sue. "Give me a second to grab my purse and lock up."

She located the key Joe had mentioned in the cabinet above the stove, slung her purse over her shoulder and, leaving the windows open for circulation, locked the door behind her as she headed down the stairs. She crossed the driveway and knocked on the side door of the house.

"Come on in!" Sue called.

The screen door squeaked on its hinges as Reily pulled it open. A rush of cool air enveloped her as she stepped into the spacious, updated kitchen. With its granite countertops, cherry cupboards and stainless steel appliances, it looked like something out of an issue of *Better Homes and Gardens*. Sue stood at the stove stirring the contents of a large silver pot. Whatever she was making smelled delicious.

"Come on in and have a seat," she said.

Reily sat at the kitchen table. From the other room she could hear cartoons playing on the television.

"Are you hungry?" she asked. "I've got a pot of chili simmering."

She was starving, actually, but she didn't want to take advantage. "I have to get back to the bar soon."

"It's white chicken chili," Sue said, clearly trying to tempt her. "It's my specialty."

Well, if it was her specialty Reily didn't want to offend her or hurt her feelings. "Maybe just a bite."

Sue spooned a generous helping into a bowl, plunked a spoon in and set it in front of her. It looked like more of a soup than an actual chili, with a white base, big chunks of chicken and several varieties of beans. Reily took a bite and her taste buds when berserk. "Oh, my gosh! This is *amazing.*"

"It's Joe's favorite," Sue said, pulling a pitcher of lemonade from the fridge. She took two glasses down from the cupboard and filled them. She set one in front of Reily, then lowered herself into the chair opposite her. "Joe tells me that you've hit a spell of bad luck."

That was putting it mildly. "I'm trying to look at it as a temporary diversion. An adventure," she said. What she was trying hard *not* to think about was all the hard-earned money she had lost, and all of her worldly possessions gone forever. It would take hard work, but she would rebuild and start over. She was tough. And she was used to getting by on very little. "I figure Nashville will still be there when I pull my life back together."

"Well, you couldn't have landed in a better place. You won't find a friendlier town than Paradise."

"If it hadn't been for Officer Jeffries and Joe and Lindy, I don't know what I would have done. I doubt anyone in Denver would have been so willing to help a stranger."

"P.J. is a good man. Though he was quite the hellion when he was a youngster. I used to babysit him when I was in junior high school. He always gave me a run for my money."

"You've lived here your whole life?"

Sue sipped her lemonade. "My great-great-grandfather was one of the founders of the town. My father built this house for my brother, Joe Senior, and the house next door for me and my husband, Walter."

"So you and your husband live next door?"

"It's just me now. Walter passed four years ago last

month, and we lost my brother Joey almost a year to the day later."

"P.J. mentioned that Joe Senior used to own Joe's Place."

"He started that bar twenty-odd years ago. I loved my brother to death, don't get me wrong. He was a good father, a good person, but a businessman he wasn't. That's why my nephew, Joey, went and got himself a degree in business. With his dad's heart problems, I think he knew that someday he would be taking over the bar. His dad would be so proud of everything he's done. Unfortunately, it just wasn't enough for Beth."

"Beth?"

Sue lowered her voice. "Joe's wife. They were high school sweethearts. But after a few years of marriage she decided she needed to *find* herself, or some such nonsense. So she just up and left." She shook her head, clucking disappointedly. "She broke that poor man's heart. Lily Ann doesn't seem to remember her much, which I think is probably a blessing. But she does realize that she's the only one of her friends without a mommy. A few don't have daddies, but that's different. A little girl needs her mother. I try to help out all I can. I retired from teaching so I could watch her for Joe, but it's just not the same."

"I was raised by my aunt," Reily told her. Sue was right. Her aunt Macie took care of her as best as she could under the circumstances, but it wasn't like having a mom and a dad. "My parents died when I was little."

"So you know what I mean."

"Aunt Sue, could I play outside?"

She turned to see Lily Ann standing in the kitchen doorway. Reily wondered how much she had heard of their conversation, if anything.

"If you stay in the yard," Sue said. "And turn off the television first."

Lily Ann darted back into the living room and the television went silent. She skipped past them, flip-flops slapping against the tile floor, letting the back door slam shut behind her as she hopped outside.

Sue sighed and shook her head. "Joe was always the cautious sort. He knew from the time he was a youngster what he wanted to do with his life. Beth was something of a wild child. Restless, you know?" She shook her head sadly. "Joe thought he could settle her, thought that once they got married and had a baby she would be content staying in our tiny little town. But that wasn't the case. And when she made her mind up to leave, there was no stopping her. Turns out she was just like my brother's wife."

"Joe's mom?"

She nodded. "She left them when Joey was a baby. I don't know what it is about the Miller men and their fascination with restless women."

"I can understand being unhappy in a marriage," Reily said. "But how does a woman leave her child?"

"I've asked myself that question about a million times. I could barely stand it when my twin sons left for college out of state. I guess sometimes people do things that don't make much sense."

"I guess." Reily checked the display on her phone and realized that it was getting late. "I better get going. I don't want to leave Lindy in a lurch on my very first day."

"How are you getting back?"

"I'm walking."

"There's a bike in the garage you could use. It's just sitting there getting dusty. Lord knows I could probably use the exercise," she said, chuckling and patting her middle. "But I do better with both my feet on the ground."

"If it's not an imposition, that would be great."

"I guess you were a little hungrier than you thought," Sue said, nodding to Reily's bowl. She'd stopped just short of licking it clean.

Reily smiled. "It was delicious. I can see why it's Joe's favorite."

They both stood and Reily grabbed her purse. "Thanks for lunch. It was really nice talking to you."

"Well, I probably told you more than you ever wanted to know about our family, but I do tend to ramble on sometimes. It used to drive poor Walter batty."

"I don't mind at all. I like hearing about other people's families. It makes mine seem not so unusual, if that makes sense."

"I think I know just what you mean. And I'm sure it's no fun being trapped in a place where there isn't a familiar face. I figured you could use a friend."

She would be honored to consider Sue her friend.

"In fact, what are you doing Sunday for supper?" Sue asked.

"Honestly, I haven't thought past five minutes from now."

"Then you'll have dinner with us. With Joe's schedule, and my Monday night poker, it's the only day we get to eat together as a family."

"I take it he works a lot."

"The bar is closed Sunday and he takes Monday off, but the rest of the week he's pretty much there open to close."

If he spent so little time with his family, Joe might not be too keen on her infiltrating their Sunday supper. "I don't want to intrude," she told Sue.

"Well," she said, planting her hands on her hips. "Since I'm doing the cooking, I get to choose the guests."

She probably should have said no. She liked the idea of spending time with Sue and Lily Ann, and maybe even Joe, but what if she got attached? She wouldn't be hanging around very long. Yet at the same time, the thought of spending the evening alone was a little depressing. She was naturally a social person. She liked to be around people. "If you're sure it's okay," she told Sue.

"Of course I'm sure."

"In that case, if there's anything I can bring, let me know. I make a mean gelatin salad."

Sue grinned. "Then definitely bring that. Gelatin is Lily Ann's all-time favorite food. Although, due to an unfortunate incident with gelatin shooters in high school, Joe won't touch the stuff. One of these days I'll tell you the story."

Reily smiled. "I'd like to hear it."

They both got up and Sue stepped out the back door with her into the blazing heat. "Lily Ann!" she called.

After several seconds Lily Ann emerged from the backyard. "Do I gotta come in *already?*"

"Do me a favor and show Reily here where that extra bike is in the garage. She's going to use it while she's in town."

"Okay, Aunt Sue."

"If you need anything," Sue said, "just knock on the door."

"Thanks, Sue."

Lily Ann darted for the garage and Reily followed her. Sue must have hit a remote inside the house because as they approached, the door rolled open.

"It's in here," Lily Ann said.

The interior was about a million degrees and smelled

like fertilizer. On one side were all the normal things you would find in a garage. Bikes, lawn equipment and tools, all neatly arranged. A car sat on the opposite side, but it was covered so she couldn't tell the make or model. Considering the size and contour she would guess something older with muscle.

She wandered over, thinking that she would take a quick peek underneath the vinyl cover. She was reaching toward it when behind her Lily Ann screeched, "Don't touch that!"

Reily jerked her hand back and turned to Lily Ann. "I was just going to peek."

"*No one* is allowed to touch Daddy's car," Lily Ann scolded, her expression so earnest, so serious.

"I just wanted to see what kind it was."

She propped her hand on her skinny hip. "You have to *ask* first, then only *Daddy* is allowed to touch it. Cars are *very* expensive."

Reily had to bite her lip to keep from grinning. She was clearly repeating verbatim what had been told to her. "I'm sorry."

She narrowed her eyes at Reily as if she wasn't sure she could trust her, looking like a miniature of her father. "Just don't let it happen again."

"I won't. I promise."

"The bike is over here."

Parked against the opposite wall were two bikes, a man's and a woman's. The woman's bike was covered in a film of dust, as though it hadn't been used in some time. It also looked as if the tires were low, but thankfully there was a bike pump hanging on the wall. The guy was just too organized.

Lily Ann watched as Reily walked the bike out onto the driveway and pumped air into the tires, then used an old towel hanging on a peg in the garage to wipe off the seat. The chain could use a greasing, but that would have to wait until later. And maybe she could take a hose to the frame to clean it up. Other than the dust, the bike didn't seem to have a mark on it. If Sue had ridden it at all, it couldn't have been more than a few times.

"I don't have a mommy either," Lily Ann said from behind her.

Taken aback by the out-of-the-blue statement, Reily turned to her. So she *had* been listening to Reily and Sue's conversation. For some reason that didn't surprise Reily. She was willing to bet that Lily Ann heard a lot of things she probably wasn't supposed to. "Your daddy told me that. It's really tough not having a mommy."

"My mommy didn't die. She left when I was three. Daddy said she isn't coming back. I asked him why, but he won't tell me."

"Maybe he doesn't know."

"I think it's because I took a long time to potty train, and she got tired of changing my poopy diapers."

The problem with not giving kids an answer to a question like that was that they had a way of fabricating one of their own. She wondered if Joe knew she felt that way, that she blamed herself.

"You know," she told Lily Ann, "I've changed poopy diapers lots of times, and it's really not that bad. Sometimes adults do things…well, that don't make much sense."

Lily Ann thought about that for several seconds, then she shook her head and said, "No, it was the diapers."

As much as she wanted to talk more about it with Lily Ann, to convince her that her mommy's leaving wasn't her fault, she felt it was neither her business nor her place

to counsel a child she barely knew. Even if they did have
the shared experience of losing a mother.

"Well, I better get to work or your daddy might fire
me," she told Lily Ann with a grin. "But I'll see you Sunday for dinner. And I'm bringing gelatin salad."

Lily Ann's eyes lit and she hopped excitedly. "Yeah!"

"What's your favorite flavor?"

"Purple!"

Grape-flavored gelatin salad. That would be interesting. "Purple it is, then," she told Lily Ann.

She climbed onto the bike, surprised that the seat
needed no adjusting, considering Sue was at least a head
shorter. She waved goodbye to Lily Ann, who waved
back enthusiastically, then she hiked her purse over her
shoulder and pedaled out into the street. She hadn't ridden a bike since she was sixteen, and she felt a little
unsteady for the first couple of blocks. By the time she
reached Main Street it was like second nature. It would
save her a ton of time walking everywhere, and maybe
Sue wouldn't mind if she attached some sort of basket to
carry her belongings. Or, she thought, as her purse slid
down her arm for the millionth time, maybe she should
invest in a cheap backpack instead.

As she steered the bike through the bar lot and behind
the building, Joe was walking from his truck to the back
door holding a jumbo-size pack of toilet paper.

With his guard down, in a more relaxed state, there
was no getting around it: Joe was a hottie. And though
she wasn't normally into the dark and brooding type, she
could make an exception for him. If she wasn't leaving
in six weeks, that is. But she wasn't any more ready to
settle down than his wife had been, and she definitely
wasn't ready to be someone's surrogate mommy.

As he reached the door, Joe glanced her way, then did

a double take when he realized it was her riding toward him. His expression went dark and his brow furrowed into a deep frown.

Uh-oh, was she late or something?

She came to a stop just before the door and hopped off the bike. She opened her mouth to apologize for taking so long, but before she could get a word out Joe growled at her, "Where did you get that bike?"

Chapter Five

Jarred by his unprovoked outburst, Reily actually took a step back, away from Joe, and he felt an instant and acute jab of guilt. What the hell was wrong with him? He really hadn't meant to sound so cross. The instant the words left his mouth, logic determined that Aunt Sue had probably given her the bike to use. Though he didn't know her well, Reily didn't strike him as the type who would wander uninvited into someone's garage and help herself to its contents.

"I didn't steal it, if that's what you're thinking," she said, looking equal parts insulted and wounded. "Sue had me over for lemonade and she said I could use it to get to work while I'm in town. If that's a problem—"

"No. No problem. Just…forget I said anything."

She was quiet for several seconds, then she looked up at him and said, "This is your wife's bike, isn't it?"

Damn. Was he really that transparent?

"It's not a big deal," he said, but he could see that she wasn't buying it.

She cursed under her breath. "I'm sorry, Joe. I just assumed from the way Sue talked that it was hers. If I had realized—"

"Forget about it," he said, feeling stupid for getting all worked up in the first place. It was a bike, for Christ's sake. And though he'd bought it for Beth, thinking that it would be fun for the three of them to take family rides together—to do *anything* as a family for a change—she hadn't used it more than a time or two. As was usually the case, there was always somewhere other than with her husband and daughter that she'd wanted to be.

"I'll take it back right now if you want."

"I said forget about it," he snapped, kicking himself when his tone made her cringe. She hadn't done a thing to him, yet here she was stuck on the receiving end of all this pent-up animosity.

Taking care to keep his tone in the pleasant conversation range, he said, "There's no reason why you shouldn't use it."

"Are you sure?"

He nodded. "It's fine, really."

She didn't look convinced. "I'm sorry, Joe."

"You have no reason to be."

"Well, I am anyway."

Which made him feel like an ogre. He could see this for what it really was…Aunt Sue's way of meddling in his business, trying to make him let go of the past and get on with his life. She had done it before. Obviously that was easier said than done.

"I wanted to tell you, I had a chance to talk with Lily Ann today," Reily said. "She's a smart little girl. I'll bet she's a handful."

He couldn't help it, a smile tipped up the corner of his mouth. That always happened when someone mentioned his baby. "She sure can be."

Reily hesitated, her plump lower lip clamped between her teeth, then she said, "Lily Ann said something to me that—"

Before she could finish her sentence the door swung open and Joe had to jump back to keep from getting clobbered. It was Jill, out for a smoke break before the dinner rush.

"Oh, there you are," she said when she saw Reily. "I don't know how they do things in Minnesota, or wherever it is you're from, but here in Paradise we show up on time for our shifts."

Boy, Reily was getting it from all sides today. His surprise at Jill's snarky tone was mirrored in Reily's face.

"Is there a problem, Jill?" he asked. Jill, who obviously had no idea he was standing there, whipped around to face him.

"Joe! You scared the crap out of me," she said, laughing nervously, her face blushing deep red. "I didn't know you were back."

"Just got here." A fact that was clearly making her uncomfortable. Probably because she was in no position to preach the virtues of being on time, since she rarely ever was. And on top of her perpetual tardiness she always took more frequent and longer breaks than she was supposed to, oftentimes lingering out back chain-smoking until someone had to come and fetch her. On top of that, she wasn't even a very good waitress. She was slow and inattentive and managed to screw up at least one or two food orders every shift. He probably would have fired her ages ago if it weren't for the fact that she was raising her son all by herself, with no financial support from the boy's deadbeat dad.

He was all set to put Jill in her place, but Reily didn't give him a chance. She met Jill's gaze directly and said in a tone that was much more pleasant than warranted given the situation, "Lindy told me to be back by four-thirty. And it's now—" she pulled her phone from her jeans pocket and checked the display "—three fifty-three. So actually I'm early."

Joe smothered a smile. Clearly Reily didn't feel she had to take any crap, but she wasn't going to lower herself to using the same snotty tone as Jill. Of course, Jill probably never would have talked to Reily that way if she knew Joe had been standing right there.

"Why don't you take this inside for me," Joe said, handing Jill the package of toilet paper. "Make sure all the stalls have fresh rolls."

She hesitated, looking longingly at the pack of cigarettes in her left hand. For a second he thought she might actually argue with him. The pile of cigarette butts on the ground next to the door said she'd smoked at least half a pack already. Finally she nodded and said, "Yeah, sure, Joe."

She yanked the door open and went back inside.

Reily shook her head. "I don't know what I've said or done to offend her, but she sure doesn't seem to like me too much."

Joe couldn't know for sure, but he had a pretty good guess. Jill had been trying for a while to get her hooks into him. Maybe she saw Reily as a threat, which was ridiculous of course. Anyone who knew him knew he would never get involved with a woman like Reily. Or Jill, for that matter. So if it was jealousy, it was wasted on him.

"I wouldn't worry about it," he told Reily. He pulled the door open. When she just stood there, he asked, "You coming in?"

She looked from him to the bike she was still clutching and said, "I just realized that I don't have a lock for this."

"Don't worry about it. Paradise is a pretty honest place. No one will steal it."

"You're sure? I just had my car stolen barely five miles from here. Because I would feel awful if someone took it."

Considering his reaction earlier, could he blame her for her caution? But Paradise wasn't the type of place where people stole bikes. "Highway crime rarely ever makes it into our little town. Besides, people watch out for each other here. Just park it next to the door. It'll be safe."

She did as he suggested and followed him inside. She went to her locker to drop off her purse and he went into his office to do the orders for next week. He didn't see her again until the dinner rush was at its peak and he came out into the bar to greet the regulars—which was pretty much anyone there. Most were locals, but a good 20 percent of his weekend summer business came in from neighboring counties. And it wasn't unheard of to get a couple or two all the way from Denver. They came for the food, above-par service and the country-western bands he hired to play every Friday and Saturday—sometimes two or three a night.

His father had never served crowds like this. Of course, the bar was half the size back then and the only food on the menu was burgers, fries and pizza. He'd never had the money or the inclination to take it to the next level. Fresh out of college with a business degree under his belt and a new position as a financial adviser, Joe implored him to apply for a business loan, to take a chance on expanding into a full-service eating establishment. He'd even worked up several business plans for him to consider, but he had resisted till the bitter end. The insurance money after his death had given Joe the means to follow through with his plan. He liked to think that it was what his dad would have wanted, that he would have been proud of him.

He often wondered if taking over the bar and essentially chaining himself to Paradise permanently was what had put the final nail in the coffin his marriage had been gradually sliding into almost from the minute they'd said "I do." Up until that point, maybe Beth had believed that there still might be more to life than being a small-town wife and mother. That they may have landed somewhere more exciting, like the West Coast she had ultimately chosen over him and Lily Ann.

Whatever her motivation, he was finally beginning to accept that her leaving had been inevitable. And although the healing process had been a slow one, and they were bound to hit some rough patches in the future, he was beginning to realize that he and Lily Ann would be okay.

As he made the rounds, stopping occasionally to chat or help deliver a food order or drink, Joe watched Reily working the bar with Lindy. The woman didn't stop moving for a second. If she wasn't filling orders she was wiping down the bar, refilling the nut dishes or chatting up the regulars sitting there, who he couldn't deny seemed pretty taken with her. Not that he could blame them.

Their eyes met and she shot him a smile so easy and sweet, he actually forgot to breathe for a second. He had to fight the urge to smile back.

"Hey, Joe!" someone shouted over the music.

He turned to find Annie, one of the servers, approaching him. "Jill's gone AWOL again and she's got three orders up."

He grumbled under his breath. He was going to take care of this problem once and for all. "I'll get her," he told Annie, heading for the back door. Just as he was reaching for the handle it opened and Jill stepped back inside.

"Oh, hey, Joe," she said cheerfully as if she'd done nothing wrong. As though she hadn't ignored countless warnings about taking too many breaks, especially during the dinner rush.

"Hand them over," he said, holding his hand out, palm up.

She blinked. "What?"

"Your cigarettes. Give them to me."

She took a step away from him, clutching the pack to her chest as though he were a thief demanding her valuables. "Why?"

"Because I'm tired of you taking unsanctioned breaks." He wiggled his fingers and she reluctantly handed them over. "From now on, when you want a smoke break you have to come to me. And every day when you get to work you're going to drop them off in my office. Understood?"

Jill nodded, then her gaze drifted past his left shoulder and her eyes widened a fraction. Joe turned to see that Reily was standing behind them.

"Sorry. I need a jar of maraschino cherries," she said, gesturing to the stockroom, which they just happened to be standing in front of.

"I'll bring them up in a minute," he said.

She nodded and, avoiding Jill's gaze, walked away. When she was gone he told Jill, who was red-faced with embarrassment, "You've got orders up and three tables who are waiting for their food."

She mumbled an apology and hightailed it into the

kitchen. He hated that he had to treat her like a disobedient adolescent, but she wasn't giving him much choice. His only other option at this point would be to fire her, but he knew she needed the job. Joe grabbed a jar of cherries from the stockroom, and on his way back to the bar, dropped Jill's cigarettes into the top drawer of his desk.

When he stepped behind the bar he handed the cherries to Reily.

"Sorry about that," she said, setting it on the counter beside the sink. "I didn't mean to eavesdrop."

"No need to apologize," he said.

"It's just that I know how embarrassing it can be to be chewed out by the boss, but it's even worse when you have an audience."

"After the way she treated you earlier, I would think you'd enjoy seeing her chewed out."

"I'm sure she had her reasons for acting that way, and I'm guessing they have a lot more to do with her being unhappy than anything I did."

She was spot-on. She seemed to have a knack for reading people.

"It doesn't bother you when people are rude for no apparent reason?" he asked her.

She shrugged. "Sure. I mean, no one wants to be disliked. But it takes a lot less energy feeling sorry for someone than it does loathing them. Besides, no one can make you feel bad without your permission. I think that's a quote from someone, but I don't know from who."

"Eleanor Roosevelt," he said. "'No one can make you feel inferior without your consent.'"

"Exactly," she said with a smile. Then a customer gestured for another drink and she was back to work, leaving him to contemplate what an unusual and intriguing woman she was.

"She's quite a girl," George Simmons, the owner of Simmons's Hardware said. He was in his usual spot at the bar, the same one he'd occupied nearly every Saturday night since his wife, Elaine, passed last year. He sipped a Heineken and snacked on hot wings while he watched the Rockies clobber the Brewers. "And I don't mean just because she's cute."

"So, you like her?" Joe asked.

George took a bite of a wing, then wiped his mouth with a napkin. "Sounds like she's got a good head on her shoulders."

"I like her, too," Wade Spencer piped in from two seats down. He'd been carrying the mail in Paradise since he had graduated high school forty-some years ago.

Joe grinned and leaned on the bar. "Maybe you should ask her out on a date."

"Prolly would if I thought she'd go out with an old fart like me."

George shot him a look of exasperation. "And you don't think Lila's going to have anything to say about that?"

Lila was Wade's wife and the mother of his six boys. Their youngest, a set of twins named Markus and Michael, had been in Joe's class from kindergarten through graduation.

"I suppose that might be a problem, too," Wade admitted with a wry grin. "But a man can dream, right?"

Joe chuckled. "Can I get either of you another beer?"

He served the men their beers, chatted up a few more customers, then donned an apron and helped out in the kitchen for a couple of hours. In addition to working at his dad's bar, he'd worked part-time in the diner as a cook during high school, and he still enjoyed working the grill occasionally.

At ten, when the dinner rush was over, he was back out in the bar greeting the second wave of customers. This was the younger, rowdier crowd. They ordered hot wings and potato skins and flocked onto the dance floor.

Around 1:00 a.m. the crowd began to thin, and at two when they closed out the register, the bar was empty. Joe wouldn't add up the receipts until morning, but he could tell by the exhaustion on his employees' faces that it had been a busy night. After everyone else had left, he discovered Reily still behind the bar, restocking for the next day.

"Leave it for tomorrow," he told her. "It's late."

"I hate leaving things unfinished," she said, looking as exhausted as he felt.

"Well, I'm getting ready to lock up, so unless you want to spend the night here…"

She grinned. "I'll finish tomorrow."

Joe waited for her by the back door as she gathered her things from her locker, then they headed out into the deserted back lot. As he had predicted, the bike was still there. He toed the kickstand up and wheeled it over to his truck.

"Um, what are you doing?" she asked, looking confused.

He lifted the bike up and laid it in the bed of his truck. "Driving you home."

"But rides to and from work weren't part of the deal," she said.

Now she was being ridiculous. "You didn't think I would make you ride home when we're leaving at the same time, going in the same direction?"

"Truthfully?" she said.

Considering how cross he'd been with her earlier, she probably had. But he wasn't nearly as much of a jerk as she probably believed. He unlocked the truck doors and said, "Get in, Reily."

He half expected a fight from her, but she must have been pretty exhausted because she didn't argue. She just hopped up into the passenger's seat and buckled up.

When he got in she asked, "Is the bar this busy every weekend?"

"In the summer," he said, starting the engine. "In the winter it slows down, especially if the weather is bad."

"You do an impressive business," she said as he pulled out of the lot. "Especially for being in a small town."

"I've been lucky."

She looked over at him. "I doubt luck has anything to do with it."

They drove along in silence for several minutes, then she said, "There's something I wanted to talk to you about. I know this probably isn't the best time...." She paused, as if she was hesitant to bring it up.

He glanced over at her. "Was Jill giving you a hard time again?"

She shook her head. "It's not about work. It's about Lily Ann."

"What about her?"

"Did you know that she blames herself for her mother's leaving?"

Her statement took him aback. How could she possibly know that? "Who told you that?"

"Lily Ann did."

"She just blurted out that she blames herself?"

"She overheard me tell Sue about my parents being dead, and when she was showing me the bike she told me that she didn't have a mommy either. She thinks Beth left because she potty trained late, and her mommy got tired of changing poopy diapers."

"That's ridiculous," he said, pulling onto his street. He wasn't buying it, and he didn't think it was any of Reily's business anyway. "I think she was pulling your leg."

"She wasn't, Joe. She was completely serious. At five, I doubt she has the maturity to joke about something like that."

He turned into his driveway, parking in front of the garage and cutting the engine. "Look, I appreciate your concern—"

"No, you don't. You think I'm full of crap and that I should mind my own business."

Well, that much was true.

"I don't blame you for feeling that way. I thought long and hard about this and decided that I needed to mention it to you. You might not believe it, but I'm not the type of person who butts into other people's lives. But Lily Ann seems like a sweet kid, and I just hate the thought of her blaming herself for something that clearly isn't her fault. Talk to her or don't talk to her, it's your choice. I just had to let you know what she said to me." She unbuckled her seat belt and shoved the door open.

"My daughter is fine."

"I hope you're right about that. Thanks for the ride."

She hopped out and headed up the stairs to the apartment. He got out of the truck and watched until she was safely inside, then let himself in the side door of the house. The television was on in the family room; Sue was lying on the couch dozing to some old black-and-white Jimmy Stewart movie. No matter how many times he told her that he could pick Lily Ann up at her place, Aunt Sue insisted that a child should sleep at home in her own bed.

"I'm home," he said.

She jolted awake and sat up, rubbing her eyes. "Goodness, I guess I nodded off. How was work?"

"Busy. How was Lily Ann?"

"Busy." She grabbed the remote and switched off the TV. "She was a little feisty this afternoon, what with the Tooth Fairy coming, so we walked into town for ice cream after supper. That wore her out. Her tooth is in an envelope on your desk in the den and there's a dollar bill under her pillow."

"Thanks."

She stood and stretched. "Well, I'm going to head home. See you at ten."

He walked her to the door. Just as she was stepping out, he said, "Hey, Aunt Sue."

She turned and looked back at him.

"Has Lily Ann ever said anything to you about Beth's leaving being her fault?"

"No, why?"

He shrugged. "It's nothing. Just something someone mentioned. I'll see you tomorrow."

He locked up behind her, then went upstairs to check on Lily Ann. He opened her door, and through the light streaming in from the hall he could see that she was curled up with her favorite baby doll and had kicked the covers all the way down to her feet. He walked over to her bed, kissed her forehead and pulled the blanket back up over her. For several minutes he stood there, watching her sleep, thinking about what Reily had told him.

He couldn't imagine her lying about what Lily Ann said, but it was possible that she'd misunderstood or that Lily Ann had been teasing her. He knew his daughter, and she had never been one to keep her feelings to herself. If she felt that way, he would have heard about it by now.

Still, there was a small part of him that wondered, what if Reily was right?

Chapter Six

Joe's Place was even more packed on Saturday night than Friday, but the bar was closed Sunday and she wasn't scheduled to work Monday, and Reily was happy to have a couple of days off. She woke late Sunday morning and because she hadn't had a chance to go grocery shopping yet, she rode her bike into town for breakfast at the diner. She parked the bike in the rack out front. As she was walking up to the door, P.J. was walking out. Reily almost didn't recognize him in casual clothes and a baseball cap. Behind him walked a younger, taller man in a deputy uniform.

"Well, good morning!" P.J. said, a toothpick wedged in the corner of his mouth. He turned to the deputy. "This is Reily, the woman I was telling you about. Reily, this is my son Nate."

"Nice to meet you, Reily," Nate said, smiling and shaking her hand. He looked like a younger, taller version of his dad. "You seem to have made quite an impression on my dad."

"He literally saved my life."

"I heard Joe gave you a job," P.J. said. "I've been meaning to stop by the bar to see how things are going."

"Really well, actually. Not only did Joe hire me, but he's letting me stay in his garage apartment. Lindy's friend Zoey gave me some hand-me-down clothes, and Joe's aunt Sue left a care package on my doorstep last night. Everyone has been so nice."

"I'm so glad to hear it," he said with a grin that made his eyes crinkle in the corners. She'd almost forgotten what a kind face he had, and she counted her blessings that he had been the officer called to the gas station that night. "I have a garage to paint today, but I'll stop by the bar on my night off and we'll have a chat."

"I'd like that," Reily said. "And it was nice to meet you, Nate."

"You too," Nate said, flashing her a dimpled smile that was just a little flirtatious. He was cute in an all-American kind of way. "I'm sure I'll see you around."

Reily pushed through the door of the diner, which was clean and well maintained, even though the décor was from an era long past. She stopped at the hostess stand, but before anyone could seat her someone called, "Hey, Reily!"

She looked over to see Lindy sitting in a booth by the window with another woman. They gestured her over. As Reily made her way past a row of booths, she recognized at least half a dozen patrons from the bar. They all greeted her warmly, as though they had been acquainted for years instead of just a day or two.

"Hey, Reily." Lindy said when she reached their table. "This is Zoey."

Zoey looked as chic and trendy as Reily would have expected. Her hair looked professionally colored and styled and her makeup was flawless. She reeked of old money.

"It's so nice to finally meet you," Reily said, shaking her perfectly manicured hand. "I can't thank you enough for the clothes."

"It's no problem," Zoey said, smiling warmly. "Why don't you join us for breakfast?"

"Are you sure? I don't want to intrude."

"Yes, sit down," Lindy said, scooting over to make room for her. "We just ordered not two minutes ago."

Reily slid into the booth beside her and Zoey signaled for the waitress, who scurried right over. She was small and wiry, with dark hair streaked with gray that she wore in a long braid down her back. If she had to guess, Reily would say she was of Native American descent. She carried a pot of coffee in each hand. One regular, one decaf.

"Reily, this is Betty," Lindy said. "She and her husband, Lou, own the diner. Betty, this is my friend Reily. She's filling in for Mark at Joe's."

"Oh, so you're the young woman who had her car stolen," Betty said, clucking sympathetically.

Word sure did travel fast. "That's me."

"Well, you couldn't have wound up in a nicer place. What can I get you, hon?"

"I recommend the French toast," Lindy said.

"I guess I'll have the French toast and a coffee," she said, flipping over the empty cup in front of her, which Betty filled promptly.

"That'll be right up," she said, rushing off to put the order in.

Reily sipped the coffee and found it surprisingly good.

The coffee in the diner in her hometown was so weak it tasted like brown water. This coffee had bite.

"So, what do you think of Paradise?" Zoey asked her.

"Everyone has been incredibly friendly and helpful. Without Joe, I'm not sure what I would have done."

"The man is yummy," Zoey said wistfully, her long, siren-red acrylic nails clicking against her coffee cup as she lifted it to her lips for a sip. "Every available woman in town under the age of forty has been trying to land him since Beth left."

"Has he dated anyone?" Reily asked.

"Not that I've heard," Lindy said. "And if he has he's somehow managed to keep it a secret, which in this town is next to impossible. If someone sneezes it's in the paper the next morning."

"I'm from a small town, too, so I know just what you mean," Reily said. "Everyone was always in everyone else's business. I couldn't wait to get away."

"And here you are, stuck in another small town," Zoey said. "How's that for irony?"

"Only for six weeks, when Mark comes back to work. By then I should have the money to get set up in Nashville."

"Lindy tells me you're a singer," Zoey said. "Do you have friends in the music business there?"

Reily shook her head. "Nope."

"Do you at least have a job lined up?"

"No again. I'm hoping to get a bartending job to pay the bills until I can find some vocal work. I'll probably have to start out as a backup singer and work my way up."

"That must be scary, starting over somewhere completely new," Zoey said, then added, "Not just once, but twice."

"Yeah, but it's worth it. It's been my dream since I was

a little girl. My mom was a singer, too. She had a beautiful voice, and she wrote the prettiest songs. She planned to leave for Nashville on her eighteenth birthday, but then she met my dad. She said it was love at first sight, and the first time he kissed her, she knew she would spend the rest of her life with him." Which she had, though no one ever expected that time to be so short.

"That's so romantic," Lindy said with a sigh. "I take it she never made it to Nashville."

"She loved him so much, she gave up on her singing career to get married."

"Are they still together?" Zoey asked.

"They died in a car wreck when I was seven. But if they had lived, I think they still would be. I remember them as being really, really happy. But then again, I was pretty young. At that age everything is sunshine and roses."

"You should ask Joe to let you sing at the bar," Zoey said. "He's always looking for new acts."

Reily shook her head. "He's done enough for me already. Besides, I don't have a backup band or even a guitar to play. Mine was stolen with my car."

"He likes you, you know." Lindy said.

Reily looked at her like she was nuts. "What? No he doesn't. He hardly said two words to me at work yesterday." Jill's son had gotten sick halfway through her shift and she'd had to leave, so Lindy'd waited tables while Joe had helped Reily behind the bar. He'd barely acknowledged her.

"Which only proves my point," Lindy said. "He ignores you so you won't know that he's attracted to you."

"Maybe if we were in eighth grade," Reily told her.

"He watches you when you're not looking."

She frowned. "He does not."

"He *does*. He can't keep his eyes off of you."

Reily had to admit that a few times she'd had the feeling that Joe was watching her, but when she turned to look he would be mixing a drink or pouring a beer or chatting with a customer. And even if he had been looking at her, she doubted it had anything to do with him liking her. He probably thought she was going to steal from the register or something, the way he thought she'd helped herself to his wife's bike.

"Could you just imagine if you two fell in love?" Zoey said, dropping her chin in the palm of her hand, looking wistful. "It could be just like your mom and dad. You could give up singing and stay here in Paradise and live happily ever after."

When hell froze over, maybe. "Unlike my mom, I'm not giving up my dream for anyone. And it's a moot point because I'm not going to fall in love with him. I don't even *like* him. He's too…*moody*."

"Yeah, but he didn't used to be that way," Lindy said. "He used to be fun and sweet. Always smiling. Losing Beth changed him, and I'm sure that if he met the right woman…" She shot Zoey a look and Reily got a very bad feeling. "He would probably be back to his sweet, easygoing old self again."

"It would be nice to have the old Joe back," Zoey said, looking from Reily to Lindy. "And Lily Ann sure could use a mommy."

Reily's bad feeling grew. "I'm not sure what you two are plotting, but it isn't going to work. I don't like Joe, and he doesn't like me."

"Plotting?" Lindy said innocently. "We're not plotting anything."

Reily wasn't buying it, but before she could push the issue, Betty delivered their food and Zoey changed the subject. After breakfast Reily parted ways with her new friends and headed down to the thrift store. Though Sue's care package had included everything from shampoo and conditioner to all the basic condiments including ketchup and mustard and salt and pepper, Reily still needed some basic necessities. And of course gelatin and canned fruit for the salad tonight. In a way she wished she'd turned down Sue's dinner offer. The idea of spending time with Joe outside of work made her a little uneasy. But Joe hadn't invited her. Sue had, and Reily was going there to see her and Lily Ann. Joe was just part of the bargain.

With her purchases tucked carefully in the secondhand backpack she'd purchased at the resale shop on Third Street, Reily rode back home around noon. As she pulled up the driveway, she hit the brakes so hard she nearly launched herself over the handlebars. There in the center of the driveway, dressed in nothing but a pair of faded, cutoff blue jeans, the sun gleaming off his bare, deeply tanned shoulders, soaping up what looked to be a fully restored, mint-condition, black 1970 Plymouth Barracuda, stood Joe. His damp hair was a little mussed, bits of foamy suds dotted his lean-muscled chest and washboard stomach, and his unshaven face only added to the sizzling, sexy thing he had going on.

Depraved and wrong as it was, her first thought was how it would feel to dip her hands into the bucket of sudsy water, then rub them all over him. Although, as a former muscle car enthusiast, it was a toss-up as to which was more drool-worthy. Joe or the 'Cuda.

She hopped off the bike and walked it up the driveway. "Nice car."

Joe barely glanced up from the rear quarter panel he'd been scrubbing. "Thanks."

"Does it have the 383 V8?"

His head jerked in her direction, brows rising in surprise. "Yeah."

"330 horsepower?"

"That's right." He dropped the sponge in the bucket and straightened, eyeing her suspiciously. "How did you know that?"

Why was it that guys thought only other guys knew anything about cars?

"I had a boyfriend who restored muscle cars. He would have loved this." She parked the bike next to the garage, then walked back down to circle the car. "Did you buy it like this or restore it yourself?"

"I restored it." He grabbed the hose and rinsed away the soap from the spot he'd just washed. "Every weekend for about five years."

She walked around to the driver's side, peeking in the window at the flawless, red leather interior. "She's beautiful. She must be fast."

"She is."

"Can I see the engine?"

Looking as though he wasn't quite sure what to make of this new facet of her personality, he opened the driver's side door, reached in and popped the latch. He lifted the hood and Reily sucked in a breath. The engine was as pristine as the rest of the car.

She leaned in to get a better look. "Is it all original?"

He shook his head. "Authentic, but not original. She was a mess when I bought her. Not much more than a shell. I picked up most of the parts from a guy in California."

She backed away so he could shut the hood. "It's really something. And you'll be happy to know that Lily Ann is incredibly protective of it. I tried to peek under the cover the other day when we were getting the bike out and she practically came unhinged."

He shook his head and broke into an honest-to-goodness smile; Reily's knees went the tiniest bit weak. "She can be a little overprotective."

"I can't imagine where she learned that," Reily said, and Joe chuckled. The deep rumble of his laugh, the warmth of his smile, made her feel all soft and gooey inside.

Okay, so maybe she didn't dislike him quite as much as she'd let on to Lindy and Zoey, but that didn't mean she *like*-liked him either.

Like-liked? What was this? Middle school? And what was it about Joe that made her want to shake her head in exasperation and simultaneously jump him?

"Maybe someday you could take me for a ride." Fully expecting him to balk at the idea, she'd said it just to prove to herself that he was in fact not at all interested in being anything but her landlord and boss.

She was both surprised and a little dismayed when he dug a set of car keys out of his pocket and jingled them. "What are you doing right now?"

He actually *wanted* to take her for a ride? Well, that had backfired miserably. "Um, nothing?"

"I'll show you how fast she really is."

"But don't you have to look after Lily Ann?"

"She's at a friend's house."

Figured. "Well, I'm sure you've probably got things to do."

"What's the matter?" he asked with a look that was pure temptation. "You afraid of a little speed?"

Was he actually *daring* her to go for a ride in his car? A woman who used to ride along for drag races down Hickory Creek Road back in Montana?

She propped her hands on her hips and leveled her eyes on him. "Honey, your car can't go fast enough to scare me."

The thrill of the challenge was clear in his eyes and the sly grin curling his mouth. "Give me ten minutes to polish it up, and we'll just see about that."

"You're on."

Looking smug, he started rubbing the streaks from the body with a cloth as she carried her backpack up the stairs. She emptied the contents and put the perishable items in the fridge, wondering what the heck had possessed her to ask for a ride in the first place. Though logically, him taking her out in his car didn't mean he liked her. If he was like most guys she'd known, he would take anyone out if it meant a chance to show off his baby. The thought eased her nerves the tiniest bit, not that she had any reason to be nervous.

And if she was so sure he didn't *like*-like her, and she didn't *like*-like him, why did she stop in the bathroom to check her hair and swipe on bubblegum-flavored lip gloss?

Because she was an idiot, that's why.

She shook her head at her reflection in the tiny bathroom mirror. It was just a ride in a car, for pity's sake, and certainly not anything to make a big deal over.

From the driveway below she heard the throaty rumble of a car engine starting and knew Joe was ready to go. Giving herself one last furtive look in the mirror and grabbing her key on the way out, she headed downstairs.

Joe sat in the driver's seat, and although she was a bit sorry to see that he was no longer bare-chested, she had to admit that in a black muscle shirt, his tanned arm resting in the open window, he looked like quite the badass.

He gunned the engine, then let it settle to a low, deep idle. Like the purr of a lion.

"Hop in if you dare," he said with that tempting smile. This was definitely a side of Joe she'd never expected. No wonder he had so many women after him. When he let down his guard, he was completely irresistible.

She walked around and opened the door. As she slid inside, the hot leather scorched the backs of her thighs.

"Buckle up," he said, shifting gears and backing *slooooowly* down the driveway. He headed down the street at a crawl, doing five miles under the speed limit.

"I'd be careful," she said, looking over at him. "At this rate you're bound to get a speeding ticket."

He just smiled and steered the car toward Main Street. He turned right into traffic, then drove straight through town past the bar—which was the farthest point in Paradise that she had been so far.

They passed a few more random houses, which looked quite a bit shabbier than the homes within the city limits, until they reached a sign that announced You Are Now Leaving Paradise. We'll Miss You! Then they were back in farmland.

A little ways up they reached a cross street with a stop sign. Joe rolled to a complete stop, despite the fact that there was no one coming from any direction, and cautiously looked both ways. He was obviously a very careful guy. A snarky remark sat on the tip of her tongue, but before the words could form he *stomped* on the gas and they shot forward like a rocket.

Reily's breath whooshed from her lungs as she was pinned back against her seat by the sheer force of his launch. She clamored for something to hold on to, both terrified and thrilled as he buried the needle on the speedometer and the wind blew her hair wildly around her head. Any faster and they might break the sound barrier!

She'd almost forgotten the thrill of speed, and this fleeting reminder of what it felt like to live fast and reckless had her heart pumping and adrenaline racing through her veins.

But as swiftly as it began, Joe backed off the accelerator and hit the brake, thrusting her forward against the seat belt. He jerked the car off to the shoulder of the road, skidding to a stop, kicking up a cloud of dust, and jammed it into park.

Her heart hammering, her breath coming hard and fast, she looked over at Joe and realized that her hand was clamped around his biceps. Embarrassed, she jerked it back. *Way to make yourself look stupid, Reily.* No wonder he'd stopped. She was holding on so tight she was probably cutting off the blood flow to his fingers. "Sorry."

"No, I'm sorry," he said, wearing a pained expression. "I didn't mean to scare you."

Scare her? That was hands-down the most fun she'd had in *years.* She couldn't recall the last time she'd felt so…alive. And she wanted more.

She looked up at him, grinned and said, "Can we do that again?"

Chapter Seven

Joe stared at Reily, dumbfounded. He must have misheard her. With her windblown hair and her wild eyes and the uneven rasp of her breath, she looked scared out of her mind. Which, despite what he'd said, had been his exact intention. He *wanted* to scare her. He wanted her to stay as far away from him as possible, because as much as he tried to deny it, as much as he didn't want it to be true, he wanted her. And he *couldn't* want her.

"You want to do it again?" he asked, just to be sure he heard her right.

She smiled and nodded, her chest rising and falling with each harsh breath, her cheeks flushed. "I can't remember the last time I had so much fun."

She thought this was *fun?*

He wasn't sure what possessed him, or even how it happened, but something must have come over him, because the next thing he knew his seat belt was off, he was leaning over the gearshift and he was kissing her. And instead of pushing him away and maybe even slapping him, she took his lead and ran with it. She slid her arms up around his neck and pulled him closer, deepening the kiss. In that instant, every feeling he'd denied, all the emotions he had spent the last two years burying deep inside of him broke free in a hot, heady rush. The sweet taste of her mouth, the softness of her face as he cupped it in his hand, her hot breath against his lips lit a fire inside him that threatened to burn him alive.

He slid his hand around the back of her neck and sank his fingers through the silky hair at the root of her ponytail. Reily moaned softly. With his other hand he fumbled with her seat belt, so he could haul her over the console and into his lap. Was it a good idea? Hell, no. And what he planned to do after he had her there, he wasn't sure. He was functioning on autopilot, his only goal to get as close to her as humanly possible.

Through a lust-drenched haze he heard someone clear his throat beside his open window. Reily must have heard it, too; they jerked away from each other like guilty teenagers caught in a forbidden embrace.

Joe looked up and saw Sheriff's Deputy Nate Jeffries standing beside his open window. Only then did Joe notice the flashing lights of the patrol car in the rearview mirror.

He cursed under his breath.

"You in a hurry to get somewhere, Joe?" Mirrored glasses obscured his eyes, but the deputy's smile was a wry one. At least he was kind enough not to mention what he'd just caught them doing.

"Sorry about that, Nate. It was the damnedest thing. My accelerator got stuck."

"Is that so?" Nate said, clearly not buying his story.

"And here I thought you might just be showing off for a pretty lady." He leaned down, peered past Joe and said, "Hey there, Reily."

She flashed him a shaky, embarrassed smile. "Hi, Nate."

"You two know each other?" Joe asked.

"We met this morning at the diner," Nate said. "And of course the entire town has heard about you giving her a job."

Of course they had. And it was a decision Joe was regretting more as each day passed. He knew from experience how it felt to be the subject of town gossip. After Beth left, it was all anyone could talk about. He'd had no idea that by the simple act of giving a stranger a job he would be thrusting himself back into the spotlight.

"I hope I don't have to point out how dangerous it is to do what you just did," Nate said. "Driving with a faulty accelerator, I mean. Suppose you lost control, or a child crossed the road on a bike. Speed limits are posted for a reason."

Nate was right. Joe wasn't a kid anymore. He knew better. His carelessness, his lame attempt to scare Reily off, had put Reily's and his own—and God only knows who else's—safety in jeopardy. And that kiss…well, he didn't even want to think about what was going on in Reily's head. What if she took it the wrong way and expected some sort of relationship out of this?

"Will you be needing my license and registration?" he asked Nate.

"Since it was mechanical failure, I'll let you go with a warning this time. But I suggest you see to that accelerator, and your lead foot, because if I catch you going so much as two miles over the speed limit, next time I won't be so nice."

"It won't happen again," Joe assured him, feeling like the idiot that he was.

Nate tipped his hat at Reily and said, "Take care, ma'am."

He turned and walked back to his cruiser. Joe leaned back in his seat and watched in the rearview mirror as Nate cut the lights, pulled onto the road and circled back into town.

He looked over at Reily and said, "So, you still want to do that again?"

Looking guilty, she said, "I guess it was a little irresponsible of us, huh?"

"I don't know what I was thinking. And I'm sorry about the other thing, too. I'm not sure what came over me."

She blinked. "You're sorry you kissed me?"

When she said it like that, with her doe eyes all big and full of hurt, it did sound pretty callous.

"I don't mean to suggest that I didn't enjoy it, or didn't want to. It's just that I wouldn't normally be so…forward. Especially when I didn't even know if you wanted me to."

"I kissed you back, didn't I?"

She sure as hell had.

"It was probably just adrenaline and lust," she said.

This time he blinked. "Adrenaline and lust?"

"Speed gives you an adrenaline rush, and adrenaline makes you act on impulses you would normally suppress. Like lust."

Her frank and honest reply surprised him. And, weirdly enough, reassured him. She was more or less saying that he wasn't responsible for his own actions. Giving him a pass. "That actually makes a lot of sense."

"And I guess it goes without saying that it was a really bad idea."

He should be relieved that she felt that way, yet somewhere deep down he felt the tickle of disappointment. And as she gazed up at him, her cheeks flush, her lips plump and glossy, all he could think about was kissing her again.

He looked away. There was something seriously wrong with him.

"We should probably get back," he said. "Lily Ann will be home soon."

"Okay. And for what it's worth, I had fun. And I really like your car."

"Thanks." He buckled his seat belt and put the car into gear. He did a U-turn and headed back into town, taking care to stay well below the posted speed limit.

Reily was quiet for several minutes, then asked, "So, what are the odds that Nate will rat us out?"

He knew that she was referring to the kissing, not the speeding. "I don't know. His ex-wife owns the beauty salon, and if he tells her, everyone will know."

"Ex-wife? He doesn't look old enough to be married, much less divorced."

"I think he was maybe four or five years behind me in school. He married young, started a family. His son Cody was in Aunt Sue's class before she retired. Cute kid."

"Well, I hope he keeps it to himself. I can just imagine how it must have been for you after…well, anyway, it would just be simpler for both of us if no one knew. And obviously it can't happen again." She glanced over at him. "Right?"

"Obviously." Was that disappointment in her eyes or was he just seeing what he wanted to see? And why would he want her to be disappointed? Because he was? Because now that he'd had a taste of her, he wanted more? Well, wanting something didn't necessarily mean it was good for him, especially when it came to the opposite sex. That was a lesson he'd learned the hard way.

"I'm leaving in less than six weeks," she said. "I have plans."

If she thought he needed convincing, she was wasting her breath. The absolute last thing he wanted was another restless woman in his and Lily Ann's lives. He'd played that game before. "And I have a daughter who needs stability."

"It would be totally unfair to her," she said.

"And confusing."

"If anything ever did happen, she could never know about it." She looked over at him. "Not that I'm saying it would, or should. Or that I even *want* it to. I just mean, you know, hypothetically."

"You mean if we're ever swept away by lust and adrenaline again?"

"Yeah, like in a life-or-death situation."

It was such a ridiculous notion, he couldn't resist asking, "Like what?"

She shrugged. "I don't know. Like if we got stuck in an elevator together."

He looked over at her, brow raised. "That's hardly a life-or-death situation."

"It could feel like it if you're claustrophobic. Are you?"

He shook his head. "Are you?"

Frowning, she shook her head. "Well, we could get trapped in a…collapsed mine shaft."

Joe pulled into his driveway, killed the engine and looked over at her. "Because, like so many other small-town men, I can't resist the allure of a deserted mine. Out of curiosity, does this scenario involve a boy named Timmy and his above-average-intelligence canine?"

She tried to look insulted, but couldn't quite pull it off. "You're making fun of me."

A smile tugged at his lips. Instead of fighting it, he let loose and laughed. "And you're making it really easy."

She pulled in a deep breath and blew it out. "I'm trying to rationalize something that isn't rational, aren't I?"

"I find that relationships seldom are." And therein lay the problem. He'd had enough irrationality to last three lifetimes. He didn't have the energy for another hopeless relationship. But it was really hard not to think about kissing her again with the taste of her mouth still fresh on his lips. Sweet and fruity. A little tangy. Then it hit him. *Bubblegum.* She must have been wearing bubble-gum-flavored lip gloss.

"Let's just agree that it's never going to happen, and be content to stay out of one another's way," he said.

"I can do that."

They unbuckled their seat belts and got out of the car.

"Well, thanks for the ride," she said. "It was…memorable."

It sure was, he thought as he watched her walk up the stairs, mesmerized by the sway of her behind, the swish of her ponytail. And it was one memory he would just as soon forget.

Oh, good Lord, could the man kiss.

Reily stood by the open window overlooking the backyard, inhaling the scent of freshly cut grass, watching a shirtless Joe cut the lawn, transfixed by the flex of his sweat-dampened, muscular shoulders as he pushed the mower back and forth in neat rows, haunted by the memory of his scent, the rasp of his beard stubble against her chin as he ravaged her mouth. She'd kissed her fair share of men, but she couldn't recall ever feeling it quite the way she had this afternoon, of ever wanting a man the way she wanted Joe. And what would have happened if Nate hadn't interrupted them? Would they have gone for it right there in his car, or maybe tumbled into the overgrown weeds off the shoulder of the road? Or would they have come to their senses before things had gone too far?

She honestly couldn't say, and that scared her half to death. It was as if, when she was with him, her common sense took a vacation.

Joe completed the last row of grass, shut the mower off and pushed it to the garage, glancing up at the window as he passed, as if he could sense her watching him. Reily jerked back, hoping he hadn't seen her. The last thing she wanted was for him to think she was pining for him. Even though she sort of was. Apparently she should have listened to Lindy that morning at breakfast when she'd said Joe liked her.

Reily leaned against the wall beside the window and sighed. The only thing she knew for sure was that the situation had *complicated* written all over it, and despite wanting him—*really* wanting him—she couldn't have him. It wouldn't be the first time she'd sacrificed for her dream of being a singer. Even if this time it felt different somehow.

She checked the time on her phone and realized that she was due at Joe's for Sunday supper in less than half an hour. And though they had agreed to avoid each other, this was different. Sue had invited her and she'd accepted, and even promised Lily Ann she'd bring purple gelatin, so it would be rude not to show up now. Besides, there was no reason why she couldn't be friends with Sue, or even Lily Ann, so long as she kept her feelings for Joe out of the equation.

At least, that was what she spent the afternoon trying to convince herself.

Reily pulled the gelatin mold out of the fridge and gave it a shake, relieved to find that it had cooled to the correct temperature. There was nothing worse than runny gelatin salad. Especially when it was purple. She flipped it over onto a plate and covered it with plastic wrap, then quickly checked her makeup in the bathroom mirror. Not that Sue and Lily Ann would care if her mascara was smeared or her lip gloss chewed away. But there was nothing wrong with wanting to look nice. Which was why she decided to change from shorts and a tank top into a floral-print peasant blouse and a short denim skirt.

It had absolutely nothing to do with trying to look good for Joe, since she was sure he probably wouldn't notice anyway. Once they had agreed to avoid each other, she was sure he'd shut his feelings off and wouldn't give her another thought.

She ran a brush through her hair until it lay in a silky blond sheet down her back, freshened her lip gloss, then grabbed her key and the gelatin and headed down the stairs and across the driveway to Joe's side door. She knocked, expecting Sue or Lily Ann to answer. Instead it was Joe who pulled the door open. He'd showered, shaved and changed into jeans and a polo shirt.

He looked down at her through the storm door screen, then at the gelatin salad, and she could swear he looked a little green. "What's that?"

"Gelatin salad. I'm here for Sunday supper."

A frown tugged the corners of his mouth down and he said, "Why?"

Wow, way to make her feel welcome. "Sue invited me."

He opened the door, but instead of letting her in, he

stepped outside and said in a harsh whisper, "This is your idea of staying out of each other's way?"

"Sue invited me the other day. I assumed she would have told you."

"She failed to mention it."

His sarcastic tone and harsh expression suggested that it was somehow her fault.

"It's bad enough we have to be stuck with each other at work. I don't think seeing each other socially is a good idea."

Could he be a bigger jerk about this? "That's fine, since I'm not here to see you."

Sue appeared in the doorway. Tied around her thick middle was an apron that said I Love Cooking with Wine. Sometimes I Even Put It in the Food. "There you are, Reily! Come on in. Supper is almost ready." She held the door open.

Ignoring Joe's blatant look of disapproval, Reily stepped inside and into the kitchen. "Something smells delicious."

"Home-fried chicken with fresh corn from the farmers' market."

She handed Sue the gelatin salad. "It's grape, just as Lily Ann requested."

Sue raised a brow. "Grape, huh?"

"With canned fruit and maraschino cherries. I guess that's what I get for asking a five-year-old her favorite flavor."

"Can I offer you something to drink? We've got beer and wine, or if you'd like to try something with a little kick, I can make you a glass of my famous spiked lemonade."

Heaven knows she could use a drink. "I think I'll try the lemonade."

"Joe, how about you?" Sue asked.

"Sure, why not," he said, looking as though he probably needed a stiff drink as well.

"Why don't you and Reily have a seat in the living room while I get everything set up," Sue said. Maybe it was Reily's imagination, but she could swear she saw a twinkle of mischief flash in Sue's eyes. Oh no, not her, too. Was *everyone* trying to set them up? Reily wasn't sure if she should feel insulted and manipulated or take it as a compliment. Sue obviously cared deeply for Joe and Lily Ann. She wouldn't want to expose him to someone she didn't like and trust.

Joe shot Reily a stern look, as if Sue's suggestion was somehow her fault, and for a second she honestly expected him to refuse. Then Lily Ann skipped into the room.

"Reily! You're here!" she bellowed, hopping excitedly. "Did you bring the purple kind?"

"I sure did," she said.

She grabbed Reily's hand and tugged. "Come on, come see my bedroom!"

"Go on up," Sue said, "I'll call you when dinner is ready."

As Lily Ann dragged her from the room, Reily glanced back at Joe, who stood with his arms folded over his chest, looking as grumpy as ever. If he was trying to make himself undesirable, it was working.

"Daddy painted my room for my birthday," Lily Ann said as she pulled Reily to the stairs. They had to pass through the living room, which had polished oak floors and was filled with slightly worn, comfortable-looking furniture. And, with the exception of a toy or two, was neat as a pin. Lily Ann's bedroom was to the left at the front of the house and across from it was what looked to be a spare bedroom. The bathroom was by the stairs and she was guessing Joe's room was at the opposite end of the hall.

Lily Ann's room was painted—surprise—purple and still smelled vaguely of new paint.

"It's very pretty," Reily told her. "Why am I getting the feeling you really like purple?"

"It's my favorite color."

"When was your birthday?"

"Two weeks ago." Lily Ann darted across the room to flop down on the bed, on top of the fairy-princess-themed comforter that was primarily purple as well. She patted the spot beside her and said, "Sit down."

Reily sat beside her. "Did you have a fun birthday?"

She nodded enthusiastically. "We had pizza and soda, and my aunt Emily got me princess paper dolls and a purple purse, and I got to go spend the night at her house and stay the *whole* next day while Daddy painted. She's an animal doctor, and she took me with her to see a litter of baby pigs. They were pink and little, and they didn't smell bad at all, and I got to hold the runt. He was *so* tiny and he wiggled in my arms! And she said that when her dog Ella has her puppies, I can come help her. But that won't be for a coupla more weeks."

"It sounds like you and your aunt Emily have fun together."

"We do stuff together a lot. She doesn't have any kids yet." She paused, then added somberly, "Or a husband."

Reily smothered a smile. Clearly someone thought that was a bad thing. "Is she your daddy's sister?"

She shook her head. "Mommy's big sister. I have lots of aunts and uncles on Mommy's side, but most of them are bad, so I don't ever see them."

She wondered how many were "lots," and what Lily

Ann meant by "bad," but she didn't ask. It felt wrong to pump an innocent child for information that frankly was none of her business. The less she knew about Joe and Lily Ann's family, the better.

"Daddy doesn't have a sister or brother," Lily Ann said. "Do you?"

"Nope, it was just me." According to her aunt, her parents tried for several years to conceive again and were looking into medical options when they died. Reily had always wished she had a brother or sister, so she wouldn't feel so alone. But now, knowing that they would be all the other had, and that might have stopped her from following her dream, she was grateful to be an only child. Someday, after her career was established, she would get married and have a family. It was definitely something she wanted. It was just a matter of timing, and at twenty-six she had plenty of child-rearing years ahead of her.

"Do you want to see a picture of Mommy?"

"Um, sure," she said to be polite. Truthfully, she didn't really care to see a photo of the woman who had decimated Joe's life. Although she couldn't deny she was just a little curious.

Lily Ann opened her bedside table drawer, pulled out a framed photo and handed it to Reily. It was a shot of Beth on her wedding day. She was very pretty in a fresh, wholesome way, much like Lily Ann, though she lacked her daughter's impish quality. She looked almost angelic in her white gown, with her naturally curly, pale blond hair pulled back and draped beneath a filmy white veil. And though she was smiling, there was something in her eyes, a sadness that seemed to suck the joy from what, for most women, was one of the happiest days of their lives.

"She's very pretty," Reily said.

"Aunt Sue says I look just like her."

"You do."

"It's time to eat," Joe said gruffly from the doorway.

Chapter Eight

Reily jolted with surprise, dropping the photo on the bed as though she'd been caught misbehaving. She hadn't even heard him come up the stairs.

"Go wash your hands," he told Lily Ann.

"Okaaay," she said with a long-suffering sigh, then she hopped off the bed and darted from the room. Reily heard her run down the stairs to the main floor.

"With soap this time!" Joe called after her, then turned to Reily, his gaze shifting to the photo.

"Lily Ann wanted to show me her mommy," she told him, picking the photo up and placing it back in the drawer. "She was very pretty."

"Yes, she was."

Reily rose from the bed, wondering if, now that they were alone, he was winding up for another lecture about the virtues of avoiding each other. Instead he nearly knocked her off her booted feet by looking her straight in the eye and saying, "I owe you an apology."

She was so stunned that for a second she didn't know what to say. Finally she managed, "You do?"

"I was rude when you came to the door. I was just surprised to see you."

"I probably should have mentioned that Sue invited me over."

"No, Aunt Sue should have mentioned it. But she probably knew that if she had I would have been angry."

Reily blinked, feeling insulted. Some apology that had been.

Her look must have said it all, because he frowned, shook his head and said, "I didn't mean that the way it sounded."

At this point she couldn't feel any less welcome, and the idea of sitting at a table with him and trying to eat made her throat close. He clearly didn't want her there, and though Sue had invited her, it was still Joe's house. She never should have come in the first place.

Feeling a ridiculous urge to burst into tears, she said, "I think I should just go."

"Reily—"

She tried to walk past him but Joe stepped in her way, trapping her in the bedroom. After what happened earlier today, she didn't like being this close to him, especially when he smelled so nice. Clean, like some sort of masculine body wash. And his face looked so smooth she had to resist the urge to cup it in her hand. Looking at him made her heart beat faster and her face feel warm, so she looked at the floor instead.

"Excuse me," she said, but her voice sounded wobbly.

"You don't have to leave."

"I want to." She tried to push past him and he wrapped his hand around her upper arm. The reaction was instantaneous. Her breath caught and her heart skipped and what felt like an electrical current zapped straight through her to her fingers and her toes and *every* place in between. Heat climbed from the neckline of her blouse up into her cheeks.

He gazed down at her, his dark eyes serious, and his grip somehow managed to be firm and gentle at the same time. "Stay."

"You clearly don't want me here," she said, hoping he would let her go before she did something really stupid like slide her arms around his neck and kiss him. And this time it had nothing to do with adrenaline. This was one hundred percent pure lust.

"I *do* want you here," he said. "That's the problem."

Their eyes locked and time ground to a screeching halt. She wanted him so much, wanted him to kiss her again *so* badly, that her heart began to race.

"Time to eat, you two!" Sue called from the foot of the stairs.

"Be right there," Joe called back, his eyes never leaving Reily's, his grip on her arm tightening the tiniest bit, as if he was afraid she might try to get away. Seconds dragged on like hours as she waited for him to do or say something. *Anything.* She wasn't sure what frightened her more, the idea that he might actually kiss her again, or that he wouldn't.

Joe's head dipped a fraction of an inch and Reily held her breath, then he mumbled a curse and dropped her arm, stepping away from her. "We can't, Reily."

Reily sucked in a deep breath, feeling so dizzy from a lack of oxygen she had to grip the door frame to keep from falling over. "I know."

"Aunt Sue is waiting for us."

She nodded and followed him down the hall, praying that her wobbly knees wouldn't give out on the stairs.

Maybe Joe had been right and seeing each other socially was a bad idea. She couldn't take this stress. The next time Sue asked her over for dinner, if there *was* a next time, she would regretfully decline. As for work, she would avoid Joe as much as humanly possible.

Reily strolled slowly down Main Street, feeling contentedly full after splurging on a roast beef dinner at the diner with Lindy and Zoey. Though her first paycheck last Wednesday had been pretty pathetic once Joe had taken out all the money she owed him, and she wouldn't get paid for another two weeks, she'd worked darned hard since she got here and felt she deserved a night out with friends. And it had been fun, even though it seemed that all Zoey wanted to talk about was Joe. But there honestly wasn't much to say since, after that kiss in his car, and almost-kiss in Lily Ann's bedroom, then that disastrously awkward Sunday supper that followed, he'd been doing an impressive job of avoiding Reily. Which was the main reason why, when Sue had invited her for Sunday supper again last night, she'd said she had other plans.

But Lindy, the traitor, had taken advantage of every possible opportunity to get them in close proximity. If they needed something from the storeroom she sent Reily, knowing she would have to pass by his office. If they needed an item ordered, she made Reily tell Joe. Not that it achieved her desired effect. Even when they were forced to interact, Joe was about as personable and warm as a robot. She never thought she'd feel this way, but she honestly preferred the cranky, brooding Joe to this new Mr. No Personality. And what made the situation about a million times worse was that the more he ignored her, the more she longed for him to talk to her. The less she saw him, the more she wanted to spend time with him.

When he was nearby her heart beat like crazy, and though she was a pretty confident person she'd started behaving like a lovesick adolescent, flubbing her words or tripping over her own feet. She had a full-blown crush on a man who would barely give her the time of day.

She was *truly* pathetic.

Which was why she was out walking up and down Main Street by herself on a Monday evening, so she didn't have to sit home alone knowing Joe was just a few yards away when it might as well have been a million miles. She walked all the way down to the bar and was heading back up when someone called to her from across the street. "Hey, Reily!"

Reily turned to see Nate in his street clothes—which tonight consisted of jeans, cowboy boots and a Tim McGraw concert T-shirt—walking toward her.

"Hey, Nate," she said, greeting him with a smile. One that he returned twofold.

He sidled up beside her, hands wedged casually in the pockets of his pants. "Where ya headed?"

She shrugged. "Nowhere, really. I just had supper at the diner with Lindy and Zoey, and I thought I would take a walk before going home."

"I'm actually on my way to the diner to meet my dad. Do you mind if I walk with you?"

"I'd like that." With his blond hair and ocean-blue eyes, not to mention the dimples that dented each cheek when he smiled, Nate was above average on the looks scale. A little clean-cut for her taste, but she was guessing by the way he always struck up a conversation at the bar when he stopped in for a beer after work, and the way he watched her serve the other customers, always smiling when she looked his way, that he was interested in her. And it wouldn't hurt to have a little distraction while she was stuck in Paradise. Right? Anything to keep her mind off Joe. And why not Nate? As long as he understood that she wouldn't be sticking around.

"You don't have Cody tonight?" she asked him, recalling that he'd mentioned having his son on the weekends. Of course he'd shown off photos of the cute, towheaded seven-year-old to her.

"I normally would, but he's in Denver with his mom this weekend visiting relatives."

As he sidestepped to let an elderly woman in one of those scooters zip past, his bare forearm brushed hers. She waited for the reaction, the sizzle of sexual attraction. Even a spark or two.

Nothing. Not even a twinge.

Well, damn. So much for *that* idea.

"So," Nate said, and she could tell by his expression what he planned to say even before he said it. "What would you think if I were to ask you out to dinner sometime?"

She sighed to herself. She wanted to like him, she really did. He just didn't...*do it* for her. "Nate, you're a really nice guy...."

He cringed and said, "Oh no, not the 'I like you as a friend' speech."

She shrugged helplessly. "Sorry."

He looked disappointed, but not devastated. "It's because of Joe, isn't it?"

"What do you mean?"

He raised his brow at her.

"Okay, I know what you mean. But what happened last Sunday, that was just..." She blew out an exasperated breath. "Hell, I don't know what that was. But we agreed that it can't happen again."

"But you like him."

What was the point in denying it? Nate had seen them kiss. And he hadn't ratted them out, so he was probably the only person in town she could trust to keep her secret. "Yeah. I do. In fact, I've never felt this way about *anyone* before. And I don't even know *why*. He's cranky and moody most of the time, and I don't even like cranky, moody men, but then he'll smile and my heart will melt. And when he touches me it's just so…" She sighed wistfully, feeling like a total dope for confessing something so personal to a guy who was almost a stranger. "I am so pathetic."

"Does he like you?"

"Yeah." That was the really tough part.

A kid on a bike shot past them and Nate had to move out of his way or get plowed down. "So what's the problem?"

"I'm leaving in less than five weeks."

"So you could enjoy each other's company until you go. What's wrong with that?"

"He's afraid Lily Ann is going to get attached, and get hurt. And frankly, so am I. She's been through so much already with Beth leaving."

"She doesn't have to know that you're anything but friends. I've dated a lot of women that Cody never even met. Yes, it's tricky to pull off living in a small town, but you can do it."

He had a point. There was no reason why Lily Ann would have to know they were seeing each other. "Maybe Joe is afraid of getting hurt, too."

"You know, just now when I asked you out, I pretty much knew you were going to say no, but that didn't stop me from trying. What's the point in life if you don't take chances?"

"I guess that's a chance he's not willing to take."

"So change his mind."

She looked over at him. "How am I supposed to do that? And why do you even care? Five minutes ago you were asking me out on a date, now you're trying to set me up with someone else?"

Nate shrugged. "Maybe I think that you two just might need each other."

"But you hardly even *know* me."

"I guess it's just a feeling I have. And my instincts have always been right on the mark. Just like I always thought that Joe made a mistake marrying Beth, and I was right about that."

They passed the ice cream shop, which in the blazing heat was overflowing with people, several of whom she recognized from the bar and said hello to. It was strange, but after only nine days in town, she almost felt as if she belonged. As if, in a weird way, she was one of them. It was…nice.

"You knew Beth?" she asked Nate.

"Not real well, but I went to school with a couple of her brothers. That whole family was bad news. Emily, the oldest, is the only one who really ever made anything of herself."

"She's the town vet, right?"

He nodded. "Her parents were so messed up on drugs and alcohol that she practically had to raise her six brothers and sisters. Her mom passed away a couple of years back from cirrhosis and her dad is doing a dime in state prison for possession with intent to distribute. Two of her brothers skipped the state with warrants against them and one died of an overdose several years ago. There's another sister but she took off when she was sixteen, and far as I know, no one has heard from her. There were reports of marital and child abuse."

"Wow."

"Yeah. They put the *fun* in *dysfunction*."

"Was Beth into drugs?"

"Not that I know of, but you can't grow up in that sort of environment without deep emotional scars. I guess Joe thought he could save her, but I honestly wasn't surprised when she took off."

"Lily Ann mentioned that people in her mommy's family were bad. Now I guess I know what she meant."

They walked along in silence for a minute or two, then Nate said, "So, if Joe really does like you, it stands to reason that it would probably irk the hell out of him to see you with another guy, right?"

She shrugged. At this point, she wouldn't begin to guess what went on in that head of his. "I have no idea."

"Well, we're about to find out."

No sooner had the words left his mouth when she heard a child shriek her name and looked up to see Lily Ann charging down the sidewalk toward her. Joe was several yards behind, walking at a leisurely pace, dressed in cargo shorts, a white T-shirt and sandals, wearing his usual somber expression.

Lily Ann launched herself at Reily and wrapped her arms around her legs. "I haven't seen you *forever!* I missed you."

It had actually only been two days, but maybe to a five-year-old that felt like forever.

"Hey, kiddo! I missed you, too. I've just been very busy with work." Reily tousled her hair, jolting with surprise when she felt Nate's arm snake around her waist. She darted him a look, but he just grinned.

Lily Ann didn't even seem to notice. "Me and Daddy are going to the ice cream shop! I'm gonna get *two* scoops of chocolate in a waffle cone."

"You're getting a sugar cone with a baby scoop," Joe said, joining them, and in response to Lily Ann's pout added, "And you probably won't even be able to finish that."

Lily Ann stuck her lip out. "Can too."

"Hey, Joe," Nate said, not removing his arm from Reily's waist. And it just felt wrong. Not creepy, sexual harassment wrong. Just…unusual. Uncomfortable.

"Nate, Reily," Joe said, nodding cordially, but his jaw looked tense and he avoided her gaze. Maybe that had more to do with her and Joe being stuck together in a "social setting" than with Nate's arm around her.

"You wanna come, too?" Lily Ann asked her, and turned to her dad, tugging on the hem of his shirt. "Can she come with us? Please, Daddy, can she?"

"I think Reily has other plans," Joe said, his gaze catching hers for an instant, then looking away.

Was that a hint of jealousy she saw in his eyes? A note of sarcasm in his tone?

"Actually, she doesn't," Nate said, grinning down at Lily Ann. "I'm on my way down to the diner to meet my dad, so she's all yours. And I know for a fact that she loves ice cream."

"Yeah!" Lily Ann screeched, hopping up and down, her pink flip-flops slapping the cement.

The look on Joe's face would have been priceless if Reily hadn't been fighting the overwhelming urge to knock Nate in the head. Maybe she didn't want to have ice cream with Joe. Did he ever consider that? What was it with everyone in town trying to set her and Joe up?

Nate turned to her, and the dimpled grin said that he was clearly enjoying himself. "I'd better go."

"Yes, you'd better," she said, hoping that her eyes conveyed the silent message that the next time she saw him he was dead meat. She wondered what the sentence was for assaulting an officer, and if it would just be garden-variety assault if he was off duty at the time of the attack.

His grin widened and he said, "See you later, babe." Then he lowered his head and *kissed* her!

It wasn't a passionate kiss. Just a quick peck on the lips. She may as well have been kissing her brother, for the supreme lack of attraction she felt. But that wasn't the point. She hadn't asked for his help, and she didn't *want* his help. What she wanted was for him and Lindy and Zoey and Sue to stop playing matchmaker. And she wanted Joe to...to...wrap his arms around her and remind her how a *real* kiss should feel.

Ugh, she was *so* pathetic.

Nate strolled off down the street, and Lily Ann grabbed Reily's hand, tugging impatiently. "Come *on*, Reily, let's *go!*"

"It looks pretty busy," Joe told her. "Why don't you run ahead and grab us a place in line."

"Okay, Daddy!" She took off down the street, bursting with pride to be entrusted with such an important task.

Reily and Joe fell into step beside each other. After several seconds he said, "So, Nate Jeffries?"

She played dumb. "What about him?"

"You looked awfully...friendly."

"We are friends. He's a nice guy."

"You kiss all your friends like that?"

She had to bite her lip to keep from smiling. He really was jealous. It was a tiny bit adorable, and a little heart-wrenching. "What are you saying? If you can't have me, no one can?"

When he didn't answer she looked over at him. He was frowning.

"Did it bother you that he kissed me?"

"Of course it bothered me," he ground out through gritted teeth. His look of surprise said he probably hadn't intended to admit it. It made her feel like a big jerk because not only was he jealous, but his feelings were clearly hurt and that was the last thing she wanted.

"It was nothing," she told him.

"It clearly was not *nothing.*"

She grabbed his forearm, feeling the muscles tighten under her fingers as she pulled him off the sidewalk and into the doorway of a closed insurance office. "No, it was *really* nothing. He only did it to make you jealous."

He frowned. "Why would he do that?"

"Because he knows I like you, and in his own misguided way he was trying to help. For reasons that make no sense whatsoever, certain people in this town seem determined to set us up."

"Aunt Sue?"

"And Lindy and Zoey and now Nate. And God only knows who will be next."

Joe leaned out of the doorway to check on Lily Ann. She was in a line that stretched all the way out the shop door.

"Lily Ann, too," he said. "After dinner last Sunday she told me that she liked you and I should ask you out on a date."

She groaned and let her head fall back against the brick. "I'm sorry."

"It's not your fault."

"Yes, it is. I should have listened to you. I never should have come for dinner, and I shouldn't be going with you to get ice cream. It's just going to confuse her."

"Or maybe it's time she learned that her daddy can be friends with a woman he isn't going to marry. Because in a town this small, avoiding each other is going to be next to impossible."

"Maybe I'm not the best person to use as an example."

"Well, if you don't *want* to be friends…"

"It's hard to be friends with someone when all you can think about when you're with them is getting them naked!"

A passing elderly couple shot her a sharp look. Embarrassment burned her cheeks, and a grin tugged at the corner of Joe's mouth.

"Would you stop smiling!" she said. "That only makes it worse."

He smiled wider. "We're adults, Reily. We should be able to control our…urges."

Should be able to, but that didn't mean they *could*. But being friends with Joe would sure beat the silent treatment and make their working relationship much more enjoyable. And she might just find that being friends with Joe would curb that insatiable sexual attraction. Maybe companionship would be enough. And maybe it would get all of the matchmakers off their backs.

"I can if you can," she said, hoping it was true.

"Friends?" he said, holding his hand out to shake hers.

"Friends," she agreed, taking it. His fingertips tickled her palm and his thumb grazed her skin in a way that made her heart skip a beat. If they were going to do this, maybe touching each other, for *any* reason, was a bad idea.

Reily pulled her hand free and checked down the street. She could no longer see Lily Ann, meaning she must have been getting close to the counter to order. "We'd better go," she told Joe.

"Yeah, or Lily Ann might actually order that double-scoop waffle cone."

They walked together down to the ice cream shop and arrived just in time to place their orders. A child-size chocolate cone for Lily Ann, a double-scoop double-chocolate chip for Joe and a single scoop of cookie dough for Reily—which Joe insisted on paying for.

All the tables were occupied inside, so they decided to eat their cones while they walked back home. They'd barely made it a block when Reily heard the out-of-tune picking of a guitar. Curious, she sought out the source and saw two boys, both in their late teens, standing outside the closed barbershop across the street. The one holding the guitar was strumming awkwardly. Clearly he couldn't play. Then she focused in on the guitar itself and the air backed up in her lungs. She gasped and her cone slipped from her fingers, landing with a splat on the pavement.

She charged across the street, mindless of the traffic, over to where the boys stood and demanded, "Where did you get that?"

Chapter Nine

Both boys jolted with surprise and recoiled slightly. The one holding the guitar jutted his chin out and asked Reily, "Who wants to know?"

"I do," she said. "That's my guitar."

They both looked at her as if she were unbalanced. "No," the one holding the guitar said. "It's definitely mine."

"But it *was* mine. It was stolen along with my car over a week ago. Look on the back. Those are my mother's initials etched in the wood. *B-E-E*. Belinda Elaine Eckardt. It was hers. My dad got it for her as a wedding present."

He shrugged as if he didn't care where it came from. "That's not my problem, lady. It's mine now. I bought it fair and square at a resale shop in Denver."

"Come on," she coaxed. "You don't even know how to play."

He puffed out his chest. "But I'm gonna learn and we're starting a band."

From the sound of what she'd heard, he didn't have a musical bone in his body.

"I'm going to Nashville to be a singer, and I need that guitar," she said.

"So get a new one," the other kid said.

"Please," she pleaded, suddenly feeling desperate to have some small piece of her past back, some link to her parents. Tears burned the corners of her eyes. "It means the world to me. My mom used to play it for me at bedtime and sing songs to me. She died when I was seven years old. It's the only thing I have left of her."

The kid holding her guitar hesitated, looking guilty, then said, "If it means that much, I guess I could sell it back to you."

Relief washed over her. "Thank you *so* much. I have…" She paused, digging through her backpack for what was left of her cash. "I have seventy-one dollars."

"Seventy-one?" he balked. "Are you kidding? I paid a hundred and fifty bucks for this."

Her heart sank. Until she made more tips this week, that was the best she could do. And she feared that if she let the guitar out of her sight, even for a second, she might never see it again.

"Here's the other eighty," Joe said from behind her, and she swiveled around to see that he and Lily Ann had followed her across the street. He must have heard the entire exchange. His wallet was out and he was holding four crisp twenty-dollar bills.

"Dude, I drove all the way to Denver for this," the kid said, his eyes on the money. "Gas alone cost at least…ten bucks. And now I have to go back for a different one."

Joe pulled out another twenty. "Gas money. Now give the woman her guitar."

The temptation was too great. The kid took the money

and handed her the guitar. She hugged it to her chest, and it took everything in her not to break down and bawl like a baby.

"Do you have the case?" she asked.

"Didn't come with one," the kid said.

She couldn't tell if he was telling the truth or not, but she didn't care. She could buy a new case. The guitar was priceless. She was supposed to be saving her money, not spending every dollar she made, and it was ridiculous to have to buy her own property, but this was worth every penny it cost.

"Thank you so much," she said to Joe after the boys had ambled off, cash in hand. "I can give you the rest out of my tips next week."

"Keep your cash," Joe said. "I'll take it out of your next check."

"Are you sure? You've done so much already."

"That's what friends are for."

And he was, she realized. He was a true friend. Him and Lindy and Zoey and Sue. They had all been there for her without reservation or question.

"You dropped your ice cream," Lily Ann said, gripping her own cone, the chocolate melting down over her fingers and onto her shirt.

"I guess I did. I just got really excited when I saw my guitar."

Lily Ann held her cone out to Reily. "You can share mine."

Reily smiled. She really was a sweet kid. "That's okay, honey. Besides, I wouldn't want it to drip on my guitar."

Lily Ann shrugged and took a lick.

"You probably want to get that home," Joe said.

She hugged it tighter. "And I'm never letting it out of my sight again."

"Reily, would you sing me a song at bedtime?" Lily Ann asked. "Like your mommy used to do?"

"Sure, honey," she said, glancing over at Joe. "If it's okay with your daddy."

He smiled down at his daughter. "Of course it's okay."

"Did Mommy ever sing to me?"

A brief frown settled between his brows before he rearranged his face into a strained smile. "Sure she did. All the time."

It was a lie, Reily could tell.

They turned in the direction of home, Lily Ann skipping ahead of them. When she was far enough away that she couldn't hear, Reily asked Joe, "She didn't sing to her, did she?"

He shook his head.

"Not even when she was a baby?"

"Lily Ann was colicky, and Beth didn't have a whole lot of patience. By the time I would get home after work, she would be stressed to her limit. She would hand Lily Ann over to me and leave."

"Where would she go?"

"Out with her friends. At least, that's what she told me. Most of her girlfriends were still single. They still had the party-girl mentality. She would stay out until 2:00 a.m., then complain the next day about how tired she was. But she would do the same thing again the next night and the next. And even when she was home, she wasn't really *there.* I was the one who gave Lily Ann her bath and her bottle and tucked her into bed."

"What about when Lily Ann got older?"

He shrugged. "Not much changed."

Which made a person wonder why she'd had a baby in the first place. She clearly hadn't been ready for the responsibility.

After a brief silence, Joe asked, "Was it true what you told those boys, about your mom's guitar being all you have left?"

She nodded. "That and a few old pictures. After they died my aunt had a huge yard sale to get rid of everything from the house."

He frowned. "That seems a little insensitive."

"She didn't have a choice. She needed money."

"Your parents didn't have life insurance?"

"My dad had a small policy through work, I guess, but my aunt said that barely covered their debts."

"The minute we found out that Beth was pregnant, I bought a policy. If something happens to me, Lily Ann will be taken care of."

"That's good. I wish my parents would have been so prepared."

"My dad insisted. It's what he did when they had me. The insurance money I got after he died made it possible for me to rebuild the bar. And I was able to afford some much-needed renovations to the house before Lily Ann and I moved in."

"Where did you live before that?"

"A little house a few streets west of here. It was small, but cozy. Beth hated it. She wanted something bigger, more modern, but it was all we could afford. She wanted a lot of things that I apparently couldn't give her." He sighed, shook his head and said, "I don't know why I just told you that."

"Because we're friends," she said. "And friends talk about things."

"There are some things that I don't talk about with anyone."

"Well, maybe you should. Maybe you need to."

"Maybe," he said, his expression completely unreadable. It was amazing to her, his ability to shut his emotions off like a lightbulb. One minute they were having an open, honest conversation, the next he was robot man again.

Oh well, baby steps.

"So, is that why you were headed to Nashville?" he asked. "To sing?"

She nodded. "I'm surprised Abe didn't mention it."

"He may have. But about two minutes into the conversation, when I got the information I needed, I started to tune him out."

"Singing is all I've ever wanted to do. It's been my dream since I was a little girl. And I know every aspiring artist probably thinks this, but I'm good enough to make it. I'm willing to do whatever it takes. Being stuck here in Paradise is just a temporary diversion."

"I'm assuming your aunt couldn't help you."

"She barely gets by on her disability."

"Is she sick?"

"She got into a bad accident when she was eighteen. She was out drinking with her friends and she wrapped her car around a telephone pole. She's been in a wheelchair, in constant pain, ever since."

"And she still raised you?"

"Yeah." They turned onto Joe's street. "My grandparents were too old, and not much better off than my aunt, really. It was her or a foster home. And since she was my mom's older sister, and my mom spent years helping their mom care for her, I guess she felt obligated to take me. And she did her best under the circumstances. She won't be winning any mother-of-the-year awards, but I had a roof over my head and food in my belly. If nothing else, it taught me how to take care of myself."

"Daddy, I'm finished."

Lily Ann had stopped walking and was waiting for them to catch up. She held out what was at least three-quarters of the cone with a dollop of ice cream left inside.

"Run on ahead and put it in the trash can," Joe called to her before turning to Reily with a grin. "Told you she wouldn't finish it."

Lily Ann darted off down the street, flip-flops slapping, but came to a stop at the foot of the driveway. For several seconds she just stood there, then she turned around and ran back toward Joe and Reily, her eyes big as saucers.

"What the heck is she doing?" Joe asked, looking puzzled.

"It almost looks as if something scared her," Reily said.

When she reached them he asked Lily Ann, "Why did you come back?"

She curled what had to be one very sticky hand in his much bigger one and said in a somber voice, "Aunt Sue looks really mad."

"What do you mean, she looks mad? Where is she?"

"On the porch, fighting with the lady."

Joe frowned. "What lady?"

"I don't know, but she yelled at her, and she only yells when someone does something that makes her really mad."

Joe's expression went from puzzled to downright worried. "Then we better go see who this lady is."

He swung Lily Ann into his arms—oblivious to the chocolate ice cream she was smearing all over his white shirt—and picked up the pace. Though she couldn't help feeling she was intruding somehow, Reily had no choice but to follow, since for now it was home for her, too. Besides, Joe's alarm, and the fact that he was trying to hide it from his daughter, worried her as well.

When they reached the house Reily saw that Sue was standing on the porch, and she did indeed look mad. But the woman she was arguing with hardly appeared a threat. She was a wisp of a thing, Sue's age or older, and looked as if a strong breeze might blow her over. Her hair was gray and close-cropped. In a gauzy skirt that brushed her ankles, a silky, peasant-style blouse and copper bangle jewelry, she looked like what Reily's aunt would have referred to as an "artsy" type.

"Aunt Sue, what's up?" Joe said, rapidly closing in on the porch.

Sue spun around, looking startled to see him.

The other woman turned too. When she saw Joe, her eyes lit and she raised a hand to her chest. "Joey?"

Joe stopped at the foot of the porch steps, still holding tight to his daughter, looking puzzled. "Yes."

He obviously didn't know her. Reily was still several yards away, but she could see that the woman's hands were trembling.

"And this is your family? Your daughter and your wife?" the woman asked.

"I'm sorry, do I know you?"

The woman took a deep, shuddering breath. "No, but you used to. A very long time ago."

"You're determined to do this?" Sue asked her. The resignation in her tone, the distress in her chubby face, gave Reily a very bad feeling.

The woman turned to her. "I told you that I am. I have to."

Sue shook her head, clearly upset by whatever it was the woman was about to reveal.

"Would someone please tell me what's going on?" Joe said.

Whatever it was, Sue obviously didn't want Lily Ann to hear because she walked past the woman and down the stairs, holding her arms out to her great-niece. "Look at you, you silly goose! You're covered in chocolate. Let's get you inside and washed up."

Lily Ann went to her and Sue carried her around to the back door. When they were out of earshot Joe looked up at the woman. "Well?"

"I'm Veronica Spenser," she said. "But a long time ago I was Veronica Miller."

The color drained from Joe's face and for a second Reily thought he might actually lose consciousness. In a voice that was so cold she wouldn't have been surprised at all to see ice form on his lips, Joe glared up at the woman and said, "Hey, Mom, where you been?"

"I don't blame you for being upset," Joe's mother said.

His *mother.* He could barely wrap his mind around the concept. "You don't *blame* me? You really want to play the blame game? Because I'm going to win, hands down."

"I didn't mean—"

"What do you want?"

"Just to talk."

How many times had he imagined this moment as a child? How many hours had he spent sitting on the living room couch, staring out the front window, hoping she would come walking down the street? He would watch for her whenever he was in town with his dad, or playing on the monkey bars at the park. Occasionally he would see the unfamiliar face of someone just passing through town, one that resembled the handful of photos his father had given him, and his heart would leap up in his throat and he would pray that this time it was her, but it never had been. How many hours he had wasted thinking about her, wishing she would come home? Now she was here and he just wanted her to go away.

"What could you possibly have to say to me after all this time?" he asked.

She took a deep breath, exhaled slowly. "I know it's a lot to ask, but I'd just like the chance to get to know you. You and your family. I've made a lot of mistakes, and I have more regrets than you can possibly imagine."

"My heart bleeds for you."

"Your daughter is adorable, and your wife is very pretty."

He didn't bother correcting her, nor did he want Reily to. His life was none of this woman's business. He turned to Reily, or at least where Reily had been standing a few minutes ago, only to find that she was gone. She must have gone up to her apartment. Not that he blamed her in the least for bailing. He would have done the same if the situation were reversed.

"I don't know what it is you hope to accomplish showing up out of the blue like this, but let's get something clear. I don't know you, and I don't want to know you, so go back to wherever you came from and leave us alone."

"I was sick," she said.

Considering her short hair and frail appearance, his guess would be cancer.

"I'm okay now, but…" She paused as if waiting for a reply.

It wasn't in his nature to be cold and uncaring, but for her he would make an exception. She hadn't done a single thing to earn his sympathy.

"I'm staying at the Sunrise Motel. And I'll stay there until you're ready to talk. As long as it takes."

"Well, have fun with that." He turned his back on her—just as she had done to him thirty years ago—and walked up the driveway to the back door, realizing, as he reached for the handle, that his fists were clenched so tight his nails cut into his palms and his fingers ached.

Aunt Sue was standing in the kitchen, looking shaken and drinking a glass of what he guessed was her famous hard lemonade.

"Are you okay?" she asked.

"To be honest, I'm not sure exactly how I feel. For all I knew, she could have been dead. In a way, maybe I liked to believe that she was. It was easier to pretend that than to accept that she just didn't want to see me."

"And now that she does? Now that she's here?"

"It's too late."

She nodded solemnly as if she completely understood. "I won't lie to you. I tried to get her to leave. She stayed away this long, I thought I could persuade her to stay gone. Dealing with that woman is the last thing you need right now."

She protected him the same way he protected Lily Ann. "I guess you couldn't."

She shook her head. "She was determined to talk to you."

"Well, she didn't get what she wanted."

"And she just gave up?"

If only. "She's staying at the Sunrise. She said she'll stay there until I'm ready to talk."

"What did you tell her?"

"I have nothing to say to her."

"She tried to pump me for information. Asked what you're doing now, if you're married. I didn't tell her anything. So I guess when she saw you with Lily Ann and Reily she just assumed you were a family. She didn't know your dad was dead either. When I told her, she looked very sad. I'm not sure why, since she hadn't even cared enough to stick around."

"She said that she was sick, but she's okay now."

"I thought she looked awfully thin, and very old considering she's barely fifty. At first I didn't even recognize her. I could swear she had some work done on her face. I can't say what exactly. She just looks…different."

"I hope she didn't upset Lily Ann," Joe said, noting that he didn't hear the television from the living room.

"She seemed fine."

"Where is she?"

"Upstairs. She wanted Reily to tuck her in."

"Reily is here?" He thought for sure she'd gone up to her apartment.

"She told me she promised to sing to Lily Ann, and of course Lily Ann was thrilled." She looked up at Joe with that telltale twinkle in her eyes. "She's really taken with Reily, isn't she?"

"Aunt Sue—"

"Oh, don't go getting all defensive. I just think it's sweet, that's all. Emily is good to her, but she's never been what you could call maternal. I think it's nice that she has someone like Reily around."

The only problem was that Reily wasn't sticking around.

"I'm going to head upstairs," he said. "You can go home."

"Are you sure?"

"I'm fine." At her look of disbelief he added, "Okay, not *fine,* but I'm not on the ledge either."

"All right, but you call if you need me."

"I will."

After she left he walked upstairs, hearing the soft

strum of Reily's guitar from Lily Ann's bedroom. Not wanting to disturb them, he stopped in the hallway just outside her door and leaned against the wall to listen. He didn't recognize the melody, but it was soft and soothing. Then Reily started to sing and his heart climbed up into his throat.

She had the voice of an angel.

It was soft and sweet and hauntingly beautiful. He stood there in the hall listening until the song ended, the last chords still lingering in the air, then he stepped into Lily Ann's doorway. Reily sat on the edge of his daughter's bed, her guitar in her lap, and Lily Ann lay curled up with her favorite baby doll, her lids heavy, hovering on the cusp between sleep and being awake. When she saw him standing there she gave him a sleepy smile. "Hi, Daddy. Is the bad lady gone?"

Reily met his gaze with a look so drenched in sympathy he wanted to cringe.

"She's not a bad lady. Just a stranger. And yes, she's gone," he told Lily Ann. "And it's time for you to go to sleep."

"Thanks for singing to me, Reily. Could you do it again tomorrow night?"

Reily smiled down at her. "I have to work, but I have Wednesday night off. How about then?"

"Okay," Lily Ann said, holding out her arms. "Hugs."

Reily propped her guitar against the side of the mattress and gave Lily Ann a hug. "Sweet dreams, sweet girl."

"'Night, Daddy," Lily Ann said sleepily, her eyes already drifting closed. Joe gave his daughter a kiss goodnight, then he and Reily walked out.

"Are you okay?" she whispered as he shut Lily Ann's door. "Do you want to talk about it?"

Talking was the last thing he felt like doing. He gestured down the hall, toward his bedroom, and she followed him there. When they were inside, he gently closed the door and pushed in the lock, then he turned to her. In the dim light from the bedside lamp, she looked like an angel, too. One who had come to save him, to show him how to feel like a whole man again. Because it had been too damned long.

"I'm sorry I didn't stay out there with you," she said softly, guilt in her eyes. "The truth is, I didn't know what to do. It was a private moment. But then I felt bad just abandoning you like that."

"It's okay." He took her guitar from her and propped it against the chest of drawers.

"Sue told me that she left when you were a baby. It must have been a shock to see her after all this time."

"To be honest, I really don't want to talk about it."

She looked around the bedroom, confused. "Then why are we in here?"

"For this," he said, then he slid his arms around her, drew her against him and kissed her.

Chapter Ten

Good heavens, did the man know how to kiss.

Reily tried to fight it. Really, she did. She knew Joe was only reacting to the emotions of the moment, that he didn't really mean to kiss her. This was just his way of reasserting his authority, of feeling power over a situation where he was powerless. And since he didn't seem inclined to slam on the brakes this time, she knew that she should. She needed to tell him to stop. But then he slid one hand up to caress her cheek while the other settled on her behind, and the feeling was so erotic, the only sound she could manage was a moan.

Joe took that as encouragement and kissed her even deeper, pulling her closer, so that she was tucked firmly against the length of his body. There was no mistaking the fact that he was just as turned on as she was. She had never been more excited, or confused or terrified, at the thought of being with a man. Never had there been so much at stake. She'd always kept her relationships casual, and up until now that had been pretty easy. With Joe it was different. He was everything she could possibly want in a man, and it would be so easy to fall in love with him. So effortless. Hell, she was already halfway there. But she simply *couldn't* fall in love with him. It wouldn't be fair for anyone.

So why were her arms sliding up around his shoulders? Her fingers tangling through his hair? Why was she leaning in closer, wrapping herself around him when she should have been letting go? Then her feet were moving, mirroring Joe's steps across the room. Her calves hit the bed, and the next thing she knew they were tumbling backward onto the mattress.

He rolled her over onto her back, his weight pressing her into the softness of the comforter. Then his hand was under her shirt, burning a hot trail of pleasure against her stomach as he slid it upward, and though she knew it was coming, when his fingers brushed the cup of her bra, she sucked in a surprised breath.

Being the cautious and conscientious man that he was, she expected him to pause, to ask her if she was okay and if she wanted to stop. Instead her reaction seemed to fuel his desire. He ravaged her mouth, cupping her breast in his palm, sliding his thigh between hers and pressing intimately. Without her consent, her body arched upward and another moan worked its way into her throat. And though she didn't mean to do it, her hands fisted his shirt, tugging it from the waist of his pants.

She had anticipated this moment, fantasized about touching Joe so many times, it was hard to believe it was really happening. When she finally put her hands on him, slid her palms across the warm, bare skin of his back, it felt so good she could have cried.

What was she *doing?* She had to remember Lily Ann and Sue and everyone else who would be hurt when the time came for her to leave. She had to stop this now, before it was too late, before they *couldn't* stop.

She turned her head, breaking the kiss. "We can't do this, Joe."

"Yes, we can," he said, trailing kisses down the side of her neck, his mouth hot on her skin. "I want to."

"Think about what you're doing, and why you're doing it."

He stopped kissing her neck, lifted his head and looked down at her. A pained expression settled on his face, then he dropped his head on her shoulder and exhaled a deep, shuddering breath. He rolled onto his back beside her and said, "You're right. I'm sorry."

She was both relieved and disappointed. He could have been like so many other men, said the hell with it and kept going. The fact that he hadn't made her want him that much more.

"I'm not sorry," she told him. "Not at all."

He looked over at her. "No?"

She pushed up on her elbow. "But I also know that if we let this happen, things are going to get really confusing. And complicated. You can't deny that if your mom hadn't shown up, this wouldn't have happened."

"She isn't my mom. She's the woman who just happened to give birth to me."

"Why did she come back?"

He pushed himself up off the bed and, just like that, the shutters on his feelings banged closed again. "I don't know and I don't care."

Of course he cared. Two of the most important women in his life, his mom and his wife, had bailed on him, and now one of them was back. He needed to talk it out, work through his feelings, but it wasn't going to be easy to get him to open up.

She sat up, straightening her shirt. "It's such a pretty night. Why don't we go sit on the porch swing?"

He narrowed his eyes at her, as though he suspected she was up to something.

She stood. "Why are you looking at me like that?"

"I don't feel like talking."

She shrugged. "Fine, then we won't talk. But I sure could go for a glass of Sue's hard lemonade. I don't suppose you know how to make it."

He folded his arms across his chest. "I might."

"Great!" She walked around the bed, giving him a wide berth just in case, and grabbed her guitar. "I'm going to take this home really quick, then I'll meet you on the porch."

"But we aren't going to talk."

"We can sit in total silence if that's what you want." She reached for the doorknob. As she turned it, the lock popped. Meaning he'd had every intention of taking their relationship to the next level, and if she hadn't told him no, they would both probably be naked by now.

Oh, boy.

Her heart wiggled its way up into her throat. She could stop right now and turn around. She could slide her arms around his neck, press her body to his, and she would probably be on her back, pinned to the mattress in seconds flat.

She imagined what that would be like, how his body would feel against hers, what it would be like to make love to him, and she started getting excited all over again.

Bad Reily.

"See you in a few minutes," she said cheerfully to hide the lust seeping into her voice, keeping her back to him so he wouldn't see the deep blush that burned her cheeks. Then before she could even think about changing her mind she hightailed it down the stairs, out the back door and across the driveway.

The faintest hint of amber sunset lit the night sky and a soft, cool breeze stirred the hot air. Crickets chirped, and from a house down the street Reily could hear the playful shrieks and laughter of kids still goofing around outside. Reily headed up to her apartment and laid her guitar across the bed. She hadn't had a chance to really look it over, but there seemed to be no damage. Though it had been miserably out of tune, it still played as well as before. She would have to get a case as soon as possible, which might mean taking a bus to Denver to find one.

Reily stopped in the bathroom, grimacing at her reflection. Her ponytail was a little cockeyed and her eyeliner smeared, but she resisted the urge to fix it. And she ignored the tube of lip gloss laying on the bathroom sink. For now it might be better if she kept herself as unattractive as possible. She didn't completely trust herself. And, despite thinking Joe had enough resolve for the both of them, that obviously wasn't the case.

By the time she made it back downstairs and to the front porch, Joe was sitting there, gently swinging, a drink in each hand. He'd changed out of the chocolate-stained shirt and into a faded Joe's Place T-shirt and his feet were bare.

"Beautiful night," she said, sitting down beside him.

"Cooling off," he observed, handing her one of the glasses.

She sipped her drink. "I'll be able to sleep with the windows open tonight."

He nodded. "Supposed to be another hot one tomorrow, though."

"I heard that."

Ugh. Is this what they had been reduced to? Talking about the weather? Well, at least he was talking about *something,* which sure beat sitting there in awkward silence.

"I think I might put in a pool," Joe said.

"That sounds fun. And you certainly have the room for it."

"Lily Ann's best friend has one and she's been bugging me relentlessly all summer that we need one, too."

"Above, or inground?"

"I'm thinking inground."

"Sounds nice." And expensive, but she had the feeling he made a pretty good living.

Joe sipped his lemonade, gazing up at the night sky. "Lots of stars tonight."

She nodded. "Yep."

He was quiet for a minute or two, gently rocking the swing, forward and back, with one bare foot. Then out of the blue he said, "She told me that she was sick but she's okay now. And she just wants to talk."

It actually took a second to realize that he was referring to his mother. She knew that if she were patient and didn't push the issue he would eventually open up, but she hadn't expected it to happen quite so fast.

"You don't believe her?" she asked him.

He shrugged. "More like I don't care."

No, he did, or he wouldn't have brought it up. How could he not? She may have abandoned him, but she was still his mother. His flesh and blood. He had to be curious.

"So she left?"

"She said she's going to stay at the Sunrise until I'm ready to talk."

"She sounds determined."

"Well, so am I."

Stubborn was more like it. Maybe he got that from her. "Wouldn't it be easier to just hear her out and get it over with?"

"Maybe if I cared what she had to say. But I don't."

Was he trying to convince Reily, or himself?

"What are you going to tell Lily Ann?" she asked.

"I'm not going to tell her anything. The last thing she needs in her life is another person who's destined to let her down."

He didn't know for sure that she would. And he would never know if he didn't give her a chance. Not that Reily blamed him for his caution. But two of Lily Ann's grandparents were dead and one was in prison. For his daughter's sake, shouldn't he at least hear his mother out? Otherwise he could be depriving his child of the only grandparent she might ever know. Of course, a bad grandparent would be worse than no grandparent at all.

Despite her feelings on the matter, Joe's life—and how he chose to live it—was none of her business. But she couldn't resist asking, "What if Beth were to show up out of the blue? Would you let her see Lily Ann?"

He hesitated, and she thought he might not answer. But then he said, "I guess it would depend on why she came back. If it was just a visit and she wasn't planning on sticking around, then no, I wouldn't let her near Lily Ann."

"What if she insisted?"

"It wouldn't make a difference. I have full custody— which was *Beth's* choice, by the way. And I refuse to put Lily Ann in a position to be hurt again."

When Reily didn't say anything, Joe looked over at her and said, "You think that's wrong?"

"What I think doesn't matter. She's your daughter and you have to do what's right."

"If you knew what we went through—"

"But I don't. My parents died, and I missed them and I was miserably unhappy, but I knew that they loved me more than anything. But if one of them had just walked away...I can't begin to imagine how much that would hurt. And that's why I would never pass judgment."

He was quiet for several minutes, then in a voice laced with regret said, "I lied to you about something."

Her heart sank a little. "What?"

"When I said I didn't know why Beth left, it wasn't true." He looked over at her, his eyes so full of pain her heart ached for him. "It's my fault that she left. I'm the reason Lily Ann doesn't have a mommy."

"Did you send Beth away?" Reily asked. "Because I was under the impression she left of her own accord."

No, what he had done was even worse.

"I pressured her into marriage," he told Reily. "She wanted to travel and see the world, but I talked her out of it. I told her there would be time for that later, after our kids were grown. I convinced her that by then we would have the money to go in style. It was a lie, though. I never had any desire to leave Paradise, and I honestly believed that once we settled down and had a couple of kids, she would be so happy that she would forget all about that other stuff."

"But she didn't?"

He shook his head. Watching Beth get in her car and drive away had been hell on earth. He'd felt as though a chunk of his soul had been ripped away, as if he would never be whole again. Those first few weeks had been torture, not knowing where she was or what she was doing. If she was safe. He couldn't eat, couldn't sleep, and Lily Ann had been beside herself. Watching her wander the house, calling for Mommy, had eviscerated his already bleeding heart.

For weeks he'd heard nothing, holding out the hope that she would be so lonely without them, so miserable, that one day he would open the door and she would be standing there, and she would beg him to let her come home. Then the large manila envelope had arrived via Certified Mail from California. Divorce papers. She didn't ask for a dime from him, and she gave him full custody of their daughter. That was the day he resigned himself to the fact that she wasn't coming back. That she wanted to cut all ties to her former life, and she was truly happier without him. Without Lily Ann.

"Deep down I knew she wasn't ready for a baby," Joe said. "But I talked her into it anyway. I had myself convinced that it would solve all of our problems, make her settle down."

"You were just doing what you thought was right."

"And in doing so I deprived my daughter of her mother. That's why I never told Lily Ann why she left. I couldn't stand the thought of her knowing it was my fault. Knowing how much she would hate me for it."

She touched his arm. "Joe, listen to me. It was *not* your fault. You may have pressured Beth to marry you, but she could have said no. The same goes for having a baby. And her choice not to see Lily Ann is just that…*her* choice."

"She's so much like her mother. Lily Ann, I mean."

"That's not necessarily a bad thing. Beth must have had good qualities or you never would have wanted to marry her."

"But I don't want Lily Ann to feel restless and unfulfilled the way Beth did. I want her to be happy."

"Then you need to teach her what Beth obviously never figured out. She needs to learn to stand up for herself. She can't let anyone, not even you, squash her dreams."

Clearly she was speaking from experience. "Who tried to squash your dream?"

"*Everybody.* My aunt and all my friends. Abe. No one believed I was good enough."

"Reily, anyone who's heard you sing knows you have the talent. Maybe they just didn't want to lose you. The way I didn't want to lose Beth."

"I guess the difference is that I didn't listen to those people who said I couldn't do it. Beth should have put her foot down and told you flat-out no, she wasn't ready for marriage and kids. The fact that she didn't is *her* problem, not yours. You have to stop blaming yourself."

In a weird way, that made sense. Maybe it wasn't entirely his fault after all. "I guess I never really looked at it like that."

"Do you still love her?"

Talk about a loaded question. "To be honest, I'm not sure if I ever did. I loved the woman that I *wanted* her to be. And I'm starting to wonder if I ever really knew her. I guess that's her fault as much as mine. She had such a rotten childhood, she was afraid to open up to anyone. And instead of trying to know the real her, I just sort of…filled in the blanks. I made her into the ideal woman for me."

"And she let you."

He nodded. "Yes, she did."

"So if she were to show up tomorrow and say that she loved you and wanted to come home, that she'd changed and she wanted to be Lily Ann's mommy again, what would you tell her? Would you give her another chance?"

"If she were truly remorseful and could prove to me

that she intended to stick around, I would let her see Lily Ann. But her and I?" He shook his head. "It's over. Since I met you, that's more clear to me than it's ever been."

"Why is that?"

Knowing it was a bad idea, and not giving a damn any longer, he reached down and took her hand, lacing his fingers through hers. "With Beth, everything was a struggle. I tried to convince myself that we were both happy, that we would be okay, but I always had the feeling that any minute the other shoe was going to drop. With you it's just so…easy. I didn't know it could feel like that."

She squeezed his hand. "I wasn't supposed to meet you until years from now, when my career is established and I'm ready to settle down. And it's not fair."

"No, it's not." Knowing it was an even *worse* idea, he let go of her hand and wrapped his arm around her shoulder instead.

Reily shifted closer, resting her head against his chest. "This is really nice, but you know that we're only making it harder on ourselves."

"I know." And right now, he didn't care. He just wanted to be close to her. He needed that connection. He had told her things tonight that he'd never confessed to another living soul, because for whatever reason she seemed to understand him. Talking to her made him feel better.

"You know what would be even worse?" he said, taking her lemonade and setting both their glasses on the porch floor.

"What?"

"If I kissed you again."

She looked at his mouth, licking her own lips in anticipation. "So why do I get the feeling you're going to do it anyway?"

And that obviously wasn't a problem because as he leaned down, she lifted her chin to meet him halfway. But just before their lips met, Joe heard a truck engine and looked up to see his ex-sister-in-law Emily parking in the street in front of the house.

Chapter Eleven

Joe would normally welcome a visit from the woman he considered one of his best friends, but tonight her timing was pretty lousy. She got out of the truck. As she walked up to the porch he could see that she was carrying something, but in the dark it was difficult to say what.

As she walked up the steps to the porch Joe stood and so did Reily. Beth looked enough like her older sister that when Joe saw Emily, he always felt a brief twinge of pain and regret. Tonight, he only felt happy to see her.

"Hey, Joe," Emily said. "And you must be Reily, the new bartender I've been hearing so much about."

"Guilty," Reily said, shaking her hand.

If Emily noticed how close they'd been sitting, she didn't let on. "Sue asked me to drop these by," she said, handing Joe what he now realized was a paper grocery bag. "Tomatoes from my garden. I would have brought them sooner but I had an emergency call at Beau's place."

"That's okay," Joe told her. "We were just sitting here enjoying the cool breeze."

"Why don't I bring those inside for you," Reily said, taking the bag from Joe. "I'd like to check on Lily Ann anyway."

"Best if you take them out of the bag and set them on the counter," Emily said. "Or they might overripen."

"I'll do that. It was nice to meet you, Emily."

"You too," Emily said. "I'm sure I'll be seeing you around."

Reily let herself in the front door. When Joe turned back to Emily, she was grinning.

"What?" he asked, knowing damn well why she was looking at him that way.

"You two looked awfully cozy."

"You don't have a problem with that?"

She looked confused. "Why would I?"

"I was married to your sister, and now I'm seeing someone new."

"Beth may be my sister, but what she did to you and Lily Ann was inexcusable. I think it's wonderful that you're getting on with your life. It's something you should have done a long time ago. I've heard only good things about Reily."

"You probably also heard that she isn't staying. As soon as she has the money she's leaving for Nashville."

"How do you feel about that?"

"It sucks. I'm probably an idiot for getting involved in a relationship that has no chance of going anywhere. And for obvious reasons I don't want Lily Ann knowing about it. She really likes Reily, but I don't want her getting too attached."

"You never know, Joe. Reily may decide to stay."

He'd like to believe that, but the odds were not in his favor. Besides, they were still getting to know each other. For all he knew, they might realize over the next couple of weeks that they were completely incompatible.

"We'll just enjoy the time we have together. Keep it casual," he told Emily.

"Sounds like a plan," Emily said, then looked at her watch. "Well, I'd better get home. Oh, before I forget, Ella is due to have her puppies in a week or so, and I promised Lily Ann I would let her help, so you may be getting a last-minute call."

"That's fine. I know she'll be thrilled." Lily Ann was head-over-heels in love with Emily's border collie, and had been hinting to Joe how cool it would be if they could bring one of her puppies home. Joe wasn't sure if she was ready for the responsibility of a dog, especially such an energetic breed.

"I'll talk to you soon," Emily said.

Joe gave her a hug and watched as she walked to her truck. A minute after she pulled away Reily stepped back onto the porch.

"I'm sorry about that," she said.

He sat down and patted the seat beside him. "About what?"

She sat down, but a foot away this time. "I'm sure she noticed how close we were sitting."

"It's okay, she's a good friend."

"You two are pretty close?"

"You could say that."

"Have you and she ever…?"

He grinned. "Do I detect a note of jealousy?"

"Of course not," she said, then a wry smile tugged at her lips. "Well, maybe just a little. Even though I know I have no right to be."

He and Emily had always been friends, but they'd become especially close after Beth left. Some people thought they would become a couple, but he'd never felt more than a brotherly love for her. "She's just a good friend and a very important person in Lily Ann's life. She's the only sibling of Beth's that we keep in touch with, so she's the only real link Lily Ann has to her mom's family."

"How does she feel about what Beth did?"

"I think she blamed herself when Beth took off. Emily more or less raised her siblings since her parents weren't exactly what you'd call dependable." Weirdly enough, talking about it didn't upset him the way it used to. He felt…*detached* somehow. Reily was the only thing that mattered tonight.

"So," he said, scooting closer to her and sliding his arm around her shoulder. "I seem to recall that I was just about to kiss you."

"I think you're right," she said, meeting him halfway as he leaned in.

Her mouth tasted sweet and tangy, and though it was tough, he forced himself to keep it slow and gentle, to keep his hands from wandering, when what he really wanted to do was carry her up to his bedroom and finish what they'd started earlier. But after a while he got used to the idea that this wasn't going any further than the front porch, and he found that he was content with just kissing her. Probably because she did it so well.

In fact, they kissed for so long that he got a kink in his neck from leaning down. Though he could have easily solved the problem by pulling her into his lap or suggesting they stretch out on the living room sofa, he knew that would be pushing the boundaries of his self-control.

So when Reily finally backed away and suggested they call it a night, he didn't push.

He walked her to the garage, stopping at the foot of the stairs.

"I know it was kind of a weird night for you, but I had a nice time," she said. "I'm glad we talked."

Oddly enough, so was he. "Thanks for listening."

She rose up on her toes and pressed a soft, brief kiss to his lips. He wanted to wrap his arms around her and really kiss her but he didn't let himself. He forced himself to keep his hands at his sides. The night had been perfect just the way it was—with the exception of his mother showing up, that is. He didn't want to spoil it.

She smiled up at him. "I would say that's the last time I'll kiss you, but somehow I doubt that would stop us from doing it again."

He had the feeling she was right. Which was all the more reason he needed to stay the hell away from her. But he didn't want to. It had been a long time since he'd felt this…happy. Maybe he was setting himself up for a huge disappointment, but he didn't care.

"For the record, I really want to kiss you again," she said. "But I'm afraid that once I get started, I won't be able to stop, and we both have to work tomorrow. So I'm just going to say good-night."

"Good night."

He watched her walk up the stairs. He stood there until she was safely inside with the door locked before he turned and walked to the house. He knew it was probably a bad idea to start something with Reily when she would be gone in four weeks, but it was too late to turn back now. And, frankly, he was tired of fighting it. He could spend the next four weeks trying to figure this out, trying to slap a label on it—were they friends, lovers, something in between?—or he could just keep it casual, let nature take its course and enjoy the time they had together.

Reily wasn't exactly sure what to expect the next morning as she steered her bike up the driveway of Joe's Place and parked it next to the back door. Last night seemed a bit like a dream, and in the harsh light of day she couldn't help but wonder if the connection she'd felt, the closeness between them, was only a figment of her imagination. What if he regarded her with the same infuriating indifference, as if last night had never happened? What if they could only be "friends" when no one else was around to see it?

She stopped at her locker to drop off her backpack. The scent of fresh coffee teased her nose as she stepped into the dining room and walked behind the bar. Lindy was already there slicing limes, a cup of steaming coffee on the bar beside her. Joe was at his usual booth, laptop open in front of him. She was tempted to go over and say hi, but she was a little afraid of what his reaction might be. It would probably be better to let him make the first move.

"Good morning," Lindy said, glancing up from the cutting board.

"Morning." She poured herself a cup of coffee.

"I understand you had a pretty exciting night after you left the diner."

For several seconds she didn't know what to say. She'd just assumed that what happened at Joe's last night was private. She'd been under the impression that the situation with his mother was something he'd shared only with Reily. But of course he would have talked to Lindy about it. They had been friends for years. She probably knew all about the situation with Beth. It was silly of Reily to think that he would share his deepest, darkest secrets with a woman he barely knew and not his best friend. And if it was silly, why did she feel so jealous? And what had he told Lindy about Reily? Did she know about the kissing?

"I take it you talked to Joe," she said, trying not to sound as defensive as she was feeling.

"You know Joe, he doesn't talk about anything. But I heard he was there."

Heard he was...? Reily frowned. Why did she get the feeling they were talking about two different things?

"I didn't even know you liked Nate," Lindy said. "Not that I blame you. The guy is a hottie."

She was talking about *Nate?* She had actually forgotten all about him kissing her last night. And though it was silly, a gush of relief washed over her.

"I don't like him," Reily said.

Lindy stopped slicing and looked over at her. "Then why were you guys making out on Main Street?"

It was truly amazing how people managed to twist the facts. "We weren't 'making out.' It was *one* kiss, and he only did it to make Joe jealous."

Lindy's brow rose. "Why ever would he do that?"

"Because he saw us—" Making out in the car? She couldn't tell Lindy that. And she couldn't admit to liking Joe. "Because he thinks..." She pursed her lips. There was no way to explain it without giving away her feelings for Joe. Which would obviously be a bad idea at this point. "It's complicated."

"Well, then, who was Joe trying to make jealous?"

Reily blinked. "What do you mean?"

"When you were making out on the porch swing." She grinned wryly. "Or was that just one kiss, too?"

Reily cringed. No, that had definitely been making out. "Do you have a network of spies following me?" she asked Lindy.

Lindy grinned and set the paring knife down. "If you kiss a guy in the middle of Main Street, people are going to notice."

"And Joe?"

"My friend Claire was visiting her parents, who just happen to live across the street from Joe, and she told me that she saw Joe kissing some blonde chick on the porch, which, believe me, is pretty big news in this town. And since you're the only blonde chick he's been hanging around lately..." She shrugged. "I put two and two together."

Reily wondered if Joe knew that people were already talking about them. And if not, how would he feel when he found out? Probably not happy at all.

"So," Lindy said. "Are you two...?" She made a suggestive, borderline obscene gesture with her fingers.

"Of course not!" Reily said, batting at her hand before Joe could see her. "It's not like that."

"What's not like what?" Joe said from behind her.

Startled, Reily spun around. "Joe, hi!" she said a little too enthusiastically.

He looked from Reily to Lindy, his brow furrowing. "Did I interrupt something?"

Lindy leaned on the bar, smiling sweetly. "Reily was just trying to convince me that, despite playing tonsil hockey on the porch swing with you last night, you two are not, in fact, knocking boots."

Joe shot Lindy an exasperated look and asked Reily, "Could I have a word with you in my office, please?"

He was upset that Lindy knew. She could see it in his face. He was going to tell Reily that they should only be friends again. Or knowing that they obviously couldn't be trusted to keep their hands off each other, maybe he would take it a step further and say they couldn't be friends either. Maybe he would even fire her.

Heart in her throat, she followed him into the back to his office. As soon as they were inside, he shut the door—which could not be a good sign—then turned to face her.

"I didn't tell her," Reily said.

"Reily—"

"Lindy's friend Claire's parents live across the street from you and she was there—Claire I mean, not Lindy—and she saw us on the porch. You know…kissing."

Arms folded, Joe sat on the edge of his desk. "Okay."

"She told Lindy that she saw you making out with some blonde chick, and since I'm the only blonde chick you've been hanging around lately.…" She shrugged. "I guess Lindy just put two and two together. And to deny it would have been a lie. And I really hate lying to people. So, she knows."

"About the kissing."

"Yes, but only on the porch," she said, aware that she was babbling and that nothing she said at this point would make any difference. Lindy knew, which meant it probably wouldn't be long before *everyone* knew. "I didn't mention the bedroom, because, I mean, obviously Claire couldn't have seen *that*."

He just sat there as if he were waiting for more, and when she said nothing—she wasn't sure what else she could say—he asked, "Are you finished?"

She nodded, bracing herself for the big letdown. For the this-isn't-going-to-work speech. Instead he reached out and took her hand, pulling her between his spread thighs. She gave a little gasp as he pulled her against him, but his lips, soft and warm over hers, muffled the sound.

Either this was his way of letting her down easy, or he wasn't so upset after all. And honestly, she didn't care, because when Joe kissed her, when he put his hands on her, she could think of nothing but how good it was, how right it felt to be close to him.

When he finally broke the kiss, she felt dizzy and weak-kneed.

"What was that for?" she asked.

He grinned and she could swear her internal temperature rose ten degrees. "I've been thinking about doing that all morning. And to be honest, most of the night."

"You have?"

His brow rose. "You haven't?"

Was he nuts? Of course she had! "I barely slept, I was so obsessed with the thought of kissing you again. I just thought you would be upset that Lindy knew. And I was afraid that maybe you would think that I told her."

"She already grilled me about it this morning when she came in. I didn't tell her any more than she already knew, which is probably why she was trying to pump you for information."

"And you're okay with her knowing?"

"It's not like we have a choice. She *does* know. Someone was bound to figure it out eventually."

"So what does this mean? Are we dating? Friends with benefits? What?"

"Definitely friends," he said, resting his hands on her hips, his thumbs hooked in the belt loops of her jeans—a rather intimate stance for two people who were "friends." Then he flashed her a sly grin. "Benefits would be nice, too."

"Lily Ann can't know."

"I agree," Joe said.

Reily couldn't stand the thought of hurting her, of getting Lily Ann's hopes up, then seeing them crushed. She worried about hurting Joe, too, but this thing between them seemed to be self-perpetuating, thriving off its own momentum. Short of leaving town today, she didn't see how either of them would be able to stop it. But that didn't mean they had to let it get out of control.

"We both need to be clear about where this is going," she said.

"What you really mean is where it *isn't* going. You're leaving."

"And you're okay with that?"

"It's not as if I have a choice."

Guilt assaulted her. "Joe—"

"I'm okay with it," he said, tightening his grip on her hips, as if he thought she might bolt. "I think...I think I *need* this. For the first time in a long time I feel as if I'm actually living my life, and not just watching it pass by."

She liked the idea that she was helping him, that because of her, he could finally get over Beth and get on with his life. That he could be happy again, because he deserved it.

"So we'll keep it casual?" she said.

He nodded. "Absolutely."

"And take things slow."

There was the slightest pause before he said, "Of course."

A loud rap on the office door made her jump. She tried to back away from Joe, so whoever it was wouldn't see them standing so close, but he tightened his grip on her hips.

"Come in!" he called. Apparently he didn't care who knew about them now.

The door swung open and Jill appeared, followed almost immediately by the stale stench of cigarette smoke. "Hey, Joe, here's my—"

She was holding out a pack of cigarettes, but when she saw Joe and Reily standing so close, she blinked in surprise and her arm dropped to her side. "Oh, s-sorry. I'll…come back later."

Jill backed toward the door, eyes averted, but she couldn't hide the jumble of emotions that crossed her face. Jealousy, anger, hurt. She obviously liked Joe. Anyone with half a brain could see the way she fawned over him, would recognize her awkward attempts at flirting despite getting shot down over and over again. And though she had never been anything but surly, and at times downright hostile, Reily couldn't help but feel sorry for her.

"What do you need?" Joe asked her, not moving his hands from Reily's hips.

"I was just, um, going to give you my smokes."

Joe slipped his thumb from Reily's belt loop and reached for the pack. "Thanks."

She stepped forward, placed them in his hand, then jerked back, as if he and Reily were infected with some horrible disease she was afraid she might catch. Then she mumbled something about getting to work and backed out of the room, shutting the door firmly behind her.

"That was awkward," Reily said.

Joe just shrugged, tossing the cigarettes onto his desk.

"You know she has a crush on you."

"I know."

"I think you may have just broken her heart."

He shrugged again. "Not much I can do about that."

Reily frowned. "I feel bad for her. She seems very… lonely. And unhappy."

Someone rapped on the door.

Joe sighed and called, "Yeah?"

This time it was Lindy, and when she saw the two of them standing so close, she grinned and said, "Well, I guess that explains it."

"Explains what?" Joe asked.

"Why Jill is in such a huff."

Joe glared at her. "Is that all you wanted?"

"Annie called. She's going to be an hour late for her shift tonight."

"Ask Renee if she can stay late."

"Will do." She left, closing the door behind her.

Almost immediately there was another knock.

Joe grumbled under his breath and said in an exasperated voice, *"Come in!"*

Ray, one of the cooks, stuck his head in. "Sorry to interrupt, boss, but the service guy is here to look at the air conditioner."

"Tell him I'll be right out."

With a grin, Ray nodded and shut the door.

"So, you think everyone knows?" Reily asked Joe.

"If not, give it about five more minutes. It was inevitable, I guess."

And he seemed to be okay with that.

"I suppose we should get to work," he said, and gave her one last, slow, sweet kiss before releasing her. "I don't suppose you're free tonight after work. Say, ten-thirtyish. Maybe we could kick back, have a beer. Fool around a little."

She couldn't imagine a better way to spend the evening. "I think we could arrange that."

He tagged her with one more quick kiss, then went out back to deal with the repair guy while she went to the bar to prep for the flow of customers that would hit the minute they unlocked the front door at eleven.

Lindy, of course, was already behind the bar and looking smug. "Didn't I say that he likes you?"

"Yes, you did."

"I knew you guys would make an adorable couple."

Reily grabbed her apron and tied it around her waist. "I think it's a little premature to be calling us a couple. We're keeping it casual." And taking it slow. But considering how quickly things had progressed in his bedroom last night, slow may not have been a realistic objective.

But she didn't want this to be just about sex. Not that she didn't think it would be great, and it's not as if she was a virgin or anything. She just didn't feel they should rush this. And she felt especially weird about them fooling around with his daughter in the house, even if they were behind a locked door.

"So, does this mean you're staying in Paradise?" Lindy asked, looking hopeful.

"No, it doesn't."

Lindy shrugged. "You say that now—"

"I'm going to Nashville. It's all I've ever wanted. All I've dreamed of. Besides, who says Joe would even want me to stay? We may get to know each other and find out that we're completely incompatible."

"And if you're not? If you fall madly in love with him?"

That was entirely possible, and the idea scared the hell out of her. "Lindy, if I don't go, if I give up my dream for him, who's to say that I won't regret it later on? Who's to say I won't do exactly what Beth did?"

Lindy frowned at the thought.

"Besides, technically, I'm the first woman he's been interested in since his divorce, which means I'm his rebound relationship. And rebound relationships *never* work."

"My parents are a rebound relationship and they've been together for thirty-six years."

"Joe is going to meet someone, Lindy. Someone who can give him what he needs. Someone ready to settle down and have a family. That's just not me. Not now."

Lindy looked as though she might push the issue, but then Renee unlocked the door and the first customers arrived. Reily was flattered that Lindy liked her enough to want her to stay in town, and if circumstances were different, and Reily was looking for a place to put down roots, Paradise would be ideal. Even if things with Joe didn't work out.

But until she had to leave, they would just have to make the best of their time together, and hope that would be enough.

Chapter Twelve

Joe hadn't seen or heard from his mother since their confrontation last Monday night. He knew through word of mouth that the "strange woman staying at the Sunrise," which was how the people in the city had been referring to her, had been popping up occasionally all over town, but was mostly keeping to herself. Which was fine with him, as long as she stayed out of his way. He was confident that it wouldn't be long before she realized that he wasn't worth the trouble—just as she had thirty years ago—and left town.

But by Wednesday of the following week, she proved to be more determined to see him than he anticipated.

"Do you know that woman?" Jill asked him just as the dinner rush was beginning to die down, gesturing to a booth near the front window.

Joe turned and looked across the dining room, cursing under his breath when he saw that his mother was sitting there. "She's no one," he told Jill.

"Well, she was asking me a whole bunch of questions about you. It was kinda creepy."

"What did you tell her?" he snapped, harsher than he'd intended.

Jill looked taken aback. "Nothing, I swear."

"Are you talking about that woman over there?" Renee asked, stopping beside them on her way to the kitchen.

"Yeah," Jill said. "She was grilling me about Joe."

"Me too!" Renee said. "I think she's that lady staying at the Sunrise."

This was getting out of hand fast.

"I'll take care of it," Joe told them, bristling with annoyance. Hanging around town keeping to herself was one thing, but he couldn't have her harassing his employees. It was annoying enough that practically everyone he knew felt compelled to comment on his relationship with Reily. If anyone learned that his long-lost mother was in town, he would never hear the end of it.

He crossed to her table. She smiled up at him and said, "Hello, Joey."

"What are you doing here?"

She looked down at the salad she'd barely touched, then back up at him. "Having dinner, of course."

She looked tired and a little pale, as if she was still recovering from whatever she'd had.

"You're not welcome here," he told her.

Unfazed, she looked around. "This is a public place, is it not?"

"You're harassing my employees."

"I would hardly call asking them a few questions harassment," she said, looking so frustratingly serene he wanted to put his fist through the wall.

His jaw clenched tight, he said, "I'd like you to leave."

"I will. Just as soon as I've finished my meal. Which is

delicious, by the way. So good that I'll be back for lunch tomorrow. Then dinner tomorrow night. Then lunch the following day…" She made a loopy gesture with one slender, finely boned hand. "You get the picture."

She was so tiny. Barely over five feet, and not much more than skin and bones. He knew from the photos his father had saved that she was slender, but he had always pictured her as taller. Reily's height, maybe. But he had the feeling she wasn't nearly as fragile as she looked.

"This isn't going to work," he said. "Whatever you came here to say, I don't want to hear. I'm not going to talk to you."

She shrugged. "We'll see."

Clenching his fists, Joe turned and walked to the bar to talk to Lindy, who had clearly witnessed the exchange.

"Hey, are you okay?" she asked him. "You look really upset."

He was sure his blood pressure was through the roof. "I'm fine."

"Joe, who is that woman?"

"No one."

"She's obviously not *no one.*"

He looked around to be sure no one was listening, then lowered his voice and said, "She's my mother."

Lindy gasped. "Seriously?"

"But I don't want anyone to know. And I especially don't want it getting back to Lily Ann. It would be too confusing."

"What does she want?"

"To talk. Or so she says. She showed up at the house last week. She said she won't leave until I hear her out. Now she's asking Jill and Renee about me."

"Does Reily know about this?"

He nodded. "Reily was with me and Lily Ann when

she showed up. She seems to believe that Reily is my wife."

Lindy looked over toward the booth where his mother still sat. "She doesn't look well."

"She said that she's been sick but she's better now."

"What are you planning to do?"

"Ignore her until she goes away."

"What if she doesn't go away? It's been more than a week already. You know people are already talking. Eventually someone is going to figure out who she really is. Maybe you should just talk to her."

He set his jaw. "I wouldn't give her the satisfaction. For thirty years she couldn't be bothered to give me the time of day. It's too late now."

Her look said that he was being unreasonable, but there was no way she could understand how he was feeling. Lindy had come from a stable, loving family. She knew nothing of how it felt to be abandoned, how deeply the pain cut. "You think you can handle things without me tonight?"

She blinked in surprise. He never left before closing, only on the rare occasion where Lily Ann was sick, but tonight he felt…claustrophobic. He needed air, time to think.

He needed Reily.

"Sure, I can handle it," Lindy said.

"Call me if you need anything." He walked to his office and grabbed his keys, nearly plowing into Jill on his way out.

"You're leaving?" she said, looking as surprised as Lindy had been.

"Lindy is in charge."

"But…" She looked past him, to his desk. "What if I want to take a break?"

Meaning, how could she smoke while he was holding her cigarettes hostage? He walked back to his desk, grabbed them from the top drawer and tossed her the pack. Frankly, he was tired of having to police her.

She looked at the pack, then back at him. "I can have them?"

"You're a grown woman, Jill, and you know how many breaks you're allowed. I'm tired of making concessions for you. There's no reason why you can't follow the rules like everyone else. You need to get to work on time, be courteous to the customers and stop screwing up your orders. Either you get your act together or I'm going to have to let you go."

She stared in openmouthed disbelief as he brushed past her to leave.

"It's because of Reily, isn't it?" she said, her voice dripping with indignation. "She told you to fire me."

Up went his hackles and his blood pressure shot into the red zone. He turned back to her. "Excuse me?"

He must have looked as furious as he was feeling because her eyes went wide and she took a step back.

"What is your problem with Reily?" he asked, taking a step toward her. She took one back, colliding with the edge of his desk. "What the hell has she ever done to you?"

Jill stood tight-lipped, her face pale. She couldn't answer; they both knew that Reily hadn't done a damned thing to her. She had never been anything but cordial to Jill, because that was the sort of person she was.

"Whatever your problem is, get over it," he ground out through clenched teeth, then he forced himself to turn and walk out before he said something he regretted.

He drove home, hands gripping the wheel so tightly that by the time he pulled into the driveway they ached.

Reily's bike was parked by the side of the garage, but when he knocked on her door she didn't answer. Disappointed, and wondering where she could be, he crossed the driveway to the house. He expected to find Aunt Sue in front of the television watching *Wheel of Fortune,* but the TV was off and the room empty.

Where the heck was everyone?

He walked to the foot of the stairs. From the floor above he could hear the sound of splashing water and Lily Ann's goofy laughter. He climbed the stairs, surprised to find not Aunt Sue giving his daughter a bath, but Reily. The tub was brimming with foamy suds, and Lily Ann wore a Santa-style bubble beard, her pale hair hanging in damp ringlets around her rosy cheeks. Reily sat on a towel on the bathroom floor beside the tub, the front of her tank top soggy. They were both laughing.

"Daddy!" Lily Ann screeched when she saw him standing there. "Look, I have a beard!"

Reily turned and flashed him a bright smile. "Hey, you're home early."

They both looked so happy to see him, the stress of the evening seemed to magically evaporate into the steamy air.

"I decided to take the night off," he told them. "Where's Aunt Sue?"

"She had a bad headache when I came by to do laundry this afternoon, so I told her I would watch Lily Ann. I hope that's okay."

"Of course it is."

"Reily took me to the park, then we ate supper at the *diner,* then we got *ice cream!*" Lily Ann gushed.

"I caved and let her get a double scoop," Reily said. "She ended up wearing most of it. Hence the bath."

"Daddy, can we go to the lake Sunday?" Lily Ann

asked, kicking her legs though the sudsy water. "Me and you and Reily? I want to show her how far I can swim."

"We'll see," Joe said. Then he asked Reily, "Could I talk to you for a minute?"

"Sure," she said. "Are you okay by yourself?" she asked Lily Ann.

Lily Ann rolled her eyes dramatically. "I'm not a *baby,* silly! I take baths by myself *all* the time."

"Well, if you need me, just call." Reily pushed herself up off the floor and followed Joe down the hall to his bedroom. He left the door open a crack so he could hear his daughter, then turned to Reily, who was wearing a look that was equal parts puzzlement and concern. "Are you okay?"

Though it had been just over three weeks since she'd walked into his life, she knew him well enough to recognize when something was wrong. Rather than try to explain, he pulled her to him instead. He wrapped his arms around her and buried his face against the side of her neck, breathing her in. "I'm good now," he said. Better than good.

She rubbed her hands up and down his back. "Did something happen at work?"

"Doesn't matter," he said.

She pulled back to look up at him. "Talk to me, Joe."

He sighed. She obviously wasn't going to let this go. "My mother came in for dinner tonight. She was asking the staff questions about me."

She didn't look surprised. "I saw her drive past the house earlier today, too, and by the park when I was there with Lily Ann. I guess she's getting tired of waiting for you to come around."

He probably should have seen this coming when she

didn't leave after the first few days. "I honestly figured she would have given up by now."

"I know this isn't what you want to hear, but maybe you should just listen to her. Let her say what she came to say and then you'll never have to see her again…if that's what you decide you want."

"Of course that's what I want. She's nothing to me. And there isn't anything she can say that will change that. Talking to her would be a waste of time."

"Promise me that you'll at least think about it." She stroked the side of his face with one soft palm. "I know you're angry, and hurt, but despite what she did to you, she's still your mother. If you pass up this opportunity to talk to her, you could regret it for the rest of your life."

He wasn't going to change his mind, but he told her, "I'll think about it."

Later. Right now, all he wanted to focus on was Reily. He drew her closer, nuzzling the side of her neck, and Reily gave a soft sigh of pleasure. They hadn't gone much further than kissing, with an occasional stroke or fondle—but always with their clothes on. She wanted to take things slow and he'd been trying to honor that, but it was getting increasingly more difficult to keep his hands to himself.

"What if Lily Ann comes in here?" she asked, her voice thick with desire. He had the feeling it was getting just as hard for her to say no.

"She won't. She's like a fish. She would stay in the tub all night if I let her." He backed her against the wall beside the door, kissed his way upward to her chin, nibbled her lips, coaxing her to open up for him. When she did, the taste of her mouth, the slide of her tongue against his, had his pulse jumping. He slipped one hand beneath the hem of her top and when his palm touched the warm, silken skin of her stomach a whimper slipped past her lips, which only made him hotter. Maybe, just maybe, she would let him get past second base this time.

He slid his hand upward until he reached the band of her bra, but the instant his thumb grazed the satiny cup, her fingers closed around his wrist and she tugged his hand from beneath her shirt.

Damn.

She laid her hands on his chest and gently eased him away. "We can't. Not while she's awake."

He blew out a frustrated sigh.

She gazed up at him with sympathy. "I'm sorry. I know it's hard."

"Well, when you kiss me that way, that's bound to happen," he said.

She looked confused for a second, and when she realized what he meant she laughed and gave him a playful shove. "*Difficult.* I meant that it's *difficult.*"

He grinned. "That too."

"That doesn't mean we can't have a little fun later, after she goes to bed."

He really hoped she meant that.

"Why don't you take a minute to cool down," she said, nodding down to the conspicuous bulge behind his fly. "I'm going to go check on Lily Ann."

She slipped out of the room and Joe leaned against the wall, giving his pulse a chance to resume its normal pace. He may have been suffering a severe case of sexual frustration but, he thought with a smile, at least he felt like a man again. Since Beth took off he had barely given a thought to sex, and recently he had begun to wonder if he was even capable of those kinds of feelings any longer. But since he started hanging around Reily, his sex drive had returned with a vengeance.

He went into his bathroom and splashed cold water on his face, then he changed out of his work clothes and into a muscle shirt and nylon shorts. By the time he was finished, Reily had Lily Ann out of the tub and into her pajamas, and they were setting up the Candy Land game on her bedroom floor.

"What color do you want to be, Daddy?" Lily Ann asked him.

He regarded Reily with a raised brow.

She shrugged. "I promised her we would play."

"What color, Daddy?" Lily Ann asked impatiently.

"Pink," he said, making her giggle.

"There *is* no pink."

"Purple?"

Exasperated, she held up the pieces. "There's red, yellow, blue and green."

He sat cross-legged on the floor next to Reily. "I can't decide. You choose for me."

She plunked the blue one down in front of him. Reily chose yellow, and Lily Ann took her usual green.

"I go first!" Lily Ann announced, pulling the first card. A double purple. She shrieked with delight, carefully counting out the eight spaces. Joe went next and pulled a red, moving ahead one space. Reily got a yellow, which moved her two spaces.

Lily Ann pulled a double purple next, while Joe and Reily got singles again, putting her considerably farther ahead. Her next turn she picked the gumdrop card, which propelled her halfway across the board.

"Do you get the feeling she stacked the deck?" he whispered to Reily. She grinned and nudged him playfully.

"*Daddy,* it's *your* turn."

Lily Ann creamed them in ten minutes flat. Despite

the fact that it was already past her bedtime, he agreed to one more game, in which Lily Ann beat them horribly again.

After they put everything away and Lily Ann crawled into bed, she asked Joe, "Could Reily sing to me?"

"One song," Joe said sternly, otherwise she'd have Reily in there half the night. He leaned against the wall beside the door, listening to her sing a song about a silvery moon hiding behind a tree and chasing a possum.

His cell phone started to ring and he checked the display. It was the number for the bar. He stepped into the hallway and answered. It was Lindy.

"Is there a problem?"

"Maybe."

He headed down the stairs, hoping this didn't mean he would have to go back into work. "What's up?"

"Mark called. He said his hand is healing faster than he thought and he'll be ready to come back to work by next week."

Joe cringed. He couldn't not give Mark his job back, yet how could he let Reily go when he'd promised her six weeks? "That is a problem."

"That's why I thought I should tell you right away. I'm sure you can work something out." She paused, then said, "Hey, I have an idea. You could fire Jill and give her job to Reily. You know Annie and Renee would be thrilled."

"You have no idea how tempting that is." And if she screwed up again he just might consider it. But for now, especially after his ultimatum tonight, he couldn't justify it.

After they hung up he sat on the couch waiting for Reily, considering his options. He could just give Reily the money she needed to get a start in Nashville. It would barely make a dent in his savings. But then there would be nothing to stop her from leaving right now, and call him selfish, but he wanted as much time with her as he could get. Three more weeks—twenty-one short days—wasn't nearly enough. The way he was feeling now, he wouldn't be happy with anything less than the rest of his life.

Besides, he couldn't see Reily taking a penny from him that she hadn't earned.

He had until next week to figure something out.

He heard the stairs creak and turned to see Reily coming down. "That had to be more than one song."

"She passed out cold in the middle of the third." She shrugged, smiling sheepishly. "What can I say, I'm a total pushover."

"Come sit by me," he said.

"I should put Lily Ann's clothes in the wash so they don't stain."

"I'll do it later," he said, gesturing her over. "Come, sit."

Reily sat next to him, under his outstretched arm, drawing her knees up and snuggling against his side. "I had a great time today. I don't remember babysitting being so much fun. Of course the kids I used to sit for were little monsters."

"Well, Lily Ann has her moments, too."

"She's an amazing little girl, Joe. She's smart and funny and sassy. And sweet. And yes, she can be a little bullheaded at times, but I think that's a good thing. I don't think you ever have to worry about someone walking all over her. She's a tough kid. She's going to know how to take care of herself. You should be proud of yourself. You're doing an amazing job raising her."

"I've been thinking a lot about what you told me, about why Lily Ann thinks Beth left. I've decided that I'm going to talk to her about it. Make sure she knows that it's not her fault. It's something I should have done a long time ago."

She gazed up at him. "What are you going to tell her?"

"I'm not sure yet. Something that's as close to the truth as she can understand. I've been so afraid that she might hate me for it, but I would rather her hate me than go on blaming herself."

"She won't hate you, Joe. You're her entire life."

"I hope you're right."

"Trust me." She dropped her head on his shoulder, sighing contentedly.

"So, you said she's sound asleep?"

She nodded. "Completely dead to the world. I guess creaming us at Candy Land wore her out. It was fun though. I haven't played in ages."

"You like games?"

"Sure."

"Well then," he said, grinning down at her. "I know an adult game we could play."

She smiled up at him. "I like the sound of that."

"And in this game, *everybody* wins."

Chapter Thirteen

Joe had been so patient, and considering that he hadn't been with a woman since his wife—which he'd admitted without even an ounce of shame or self-consciousness—the waiting had to have been torture for him. Reily knew, because it hadn't been even close to that long for her and it was getting harder and harder to tell him no. Which was probably why she let him talk her into going up to his bedroom this time instead of fooling around on the couch like they usually did. And the fact that he was nibbling her earlobe when he made the suggestion, and her ears just so happened to be one of the most sensitive spots on her body—and he damn well knew it—probably had a lot to do with her caving so easily.

"We can lock the door. That way if Lily Ann does wake up there won't be any risk that she'll catch us," he reasoned, pulling her up off the couch and leading her toward the stairs. "And I swear I won't pressure you. We won't do anything more than what you're ready for."

In theory it did seem the most reasonable and safest option. The only problem was, now that they were lying on his bed with the door locked, and there was no chance whatsoever of being caught, and they were kissing and touching, and he was telling her she was beautiful, she didn't *want* to stop. She wanted to put her hands all over him. Knowing how much Beth had hurt him, how insecure her leaving must have left him, she wanted him to know, without any doubt, how attractive and sexy he was. How much she wanted him.

So when he eased her shirt up over her head, unhooked her bra and slipped it off, then pulled his own shirt off, she told herself that as long as they stopped there, it would be okay. She knew that every step closer they took to making love was a step they couldn't reverse. And maybe Lily Ann couldn't catch them, but that didn't change the fact that she was there. And having sex with a man while his five-year-old daughter slept down the hall just seemed unscrupulous.

But then Joe was kissing her, and touching her, and in her estrogen-soaked brain the line of morality started to go all gray and fuzzy.

As long as we keep it above the waist, she told herself, which was ironically an instant before she felt his hand on her inner thigh.

Bad, her brain scolded, *this is very bad.* The problem was that it didn't *feel* bad. It felt really good. Which was why, instead of telling him to stop when his hand slid upward, over the crotch of her shorts, a whimper came out instead.

Okay, so maybe it wasn't that bad, as long as he didn't go further than touching the outside of her shorts. Or at least the top of her panties, she reasoned, as he tugged the snap on her shorts free, slid the zipper down and slipped his hand inside…. Bypassing her panties altogether and going straight for the gold.

She moaned and arched against his hand and Joe mumbled in a hoarse voice, something about her being wet, which she didn't doubt was true. She was so hot for him, so turned on, the ache between her thighs so acutely intense, she could barely breathe. And thank goodness Joe didn't have a zipper or snap to fumble with, just a narrow elastic waistband. Underwear wasn't an impediment either since he wasn't actually wearing any.

Her hand closed around his erection, thick and silky and hot, and Joe hissed out a breath. Knowing that it had been so long for him, and that she would be the first, that he trusted her, wanted *her,* made her wish that things were different, that she could stay here forever. Be the woman he deserved. Until she had to go, she would try to be. She wished she could give him everything he needed and more. She just hoped that was the right thing to do. What he needed.

You're overthinking this, she told herself. *Just go with it. Enjoy it while you can.*

Then Joe moaned and shuddered in her arms, and she stopped thinking altogether.

Reily was still asleep when she became aware of Joe curled up behind her, his hand cupping her breast, the heat of his chest warming her bare back.

Nice.

She couldn't recall actually falling asleep, but obviously they must have. As good as it felt to be snuggled close to him, to feel his arm draped across her waist and his warm breath on the back of her neck, she needed to go. Fooling around behind a locked door was one thing, but spending the night was out of the question.

She pried open her eyes, confused as to why the room looked so bright. Had they left a light on? She eased out from under Joe's arm so she wouldn't wake him and leaned over to get a glimpse of the digital clock on the bedside table.

Her heart nearly stopped. Eight-fifteen?

That couldn't be right.

She blinked and rubbed her eyes, blinked again, looking over just in time to see the digital readout switch to eight-sixteen.

They'd slept *all* night?

Her heart slithered down to her knees. How could she have let this happen? How could she have been so careless? She could only hope that Lily Ann was a late riser and still in bed. And if she was awake, how was Reily going to explain the fact that she'd been in Daddy's bedroom all night?

She looked around for her clothes. She found the tank top on the floor beside the bed, but her bra seemed to have vanished into thin air. She would have to look for it later. She needed to make a quick escape.

She pulled her shirt on, cringing when she noticed her reflection in the mirror above the dresser. Her hair was disheveled and her eyeliner smeared. But it wasn't as if anyone was going to see her that way. She crept to the door, pressing her ear against it, listening for the sound of the television from the living room. When she didn't hear anything, she turned the knob, wincing as the lock released with a loud snap that seemed to echo through the silence. She peered out into the hallway, her knees going weak with relief when she saw that Lily Ann's bedroom door was still closed.

She could still slip out unnoticed.

She padded across the hall in bare feet and down the

stairs. She cringed as the floor creaked and moaned with each step. She breathed a sigh of relief when she reached the bottom undetected and dashed for the kitchen, stopping dead in her tracks when she saw Sue standing at the sink, filling the coffeepot with tap water.

Sue must have heard someone come down the stairs because she said, "Good morning." Then she turned, blinking in surprise when she saw that it was not Lily Ann or Joe, who she would naturally have been expecting, but Reily.

A witness to her walk of shame. *Wonderful.*

Reily folded her arms across her chest, hoping to cover the fact that she wasn't wearing a bra, when really, that was the least of her problems. "This is not how it looks."

Sue looked past her, smiled and said, "Good morning, Lily Ann."

Reily turned to find Lily Ann standing behind her, still in her pajamas, rubbing her eyes. When she noticed Reily standing there, she smiled. "Hi, Reily!"

Holy crap, talk about cutting it close.

"Are you watching me again today?" Lily Ann asked.

"I wish I could, honey, but I have to work today."

"Then why did you come over?"

"Um…" She didn't know what to say, what sort of fib would sound plausible to a five-year-old, especially one as smart as Lily Ann.

"Reily came over to have breakfast with us," Sue said, giving Reily a wink. "Isn't that nice?"

"Cool," Lily Ann said with a sleepy smile. She didn't seem to notice that Reily was wearing the same clothes she'd had on yesterday or the fact that she looked as if she'd just rolled out of bed. "Can we have waffles? The blueberry kind."

"Sure, sweetie. Why don't you go watch cartoons while I fix them."

"Can I have juice?"

Sue poured juice into a plastic cup and handed it to Lily Ann, who shuffled off to the living room. A few seconds later Reily heard the television switch on.

"Thank you," Reily told Sue. "I had no idea what to tell her."

"Well, now you have to stay," Sue said, gesturing to the kitchen table. "Have a seat."

"I can imagine what you're thinking right now," Reily said, sitting down.

Sue poured the water into the coffeemaker. "I'm thinking that whatever Joe chooses to do in the privacy of his bedroom is none of my business."

"I just don't want you to think that I'm…you know, slutty."

She pulled a filter and a can of coffee from the cupboard. "Then you shouldn't worry, because I don't think that at all."

"We're not sleeping together." She frowned and added, "Okay, so we did sleep, we just didn't *sleep together*. If that makes sense."

"Not really," she said, measuring the grounds into the filter. "But like I said, it's none of my business."

And the more Reily tried to explain herself, the guiltier she was sounding. She just didn't want Sue to think that she had anything but Lily Ann's best interest in mind.

"Good morning."

Reily turned to see Joe standing in the kitchen doorway. He was dressed in the same shorts as the night before, dark stubble shadowed his jaw and his hair was smashed flat on the left side of his head. He looked *adorable*.

"Good morning," Sue said, opening the freezer and peering inside. "Would you look at that, we're out of waffles. I'd better go down to the basement and grab another box from the chest freezer. And maybe I'll throw a load of laundry in while I'm down there."

"Lily Ann's clothes are by the washer," Reily said. "We had ice cream. I meant to wash them last night." Until *someone* had talked her out of it, she thought, shooting Joe a look.

"I'll take care of it," Sue said, disappearing down the stairs.

"You're here early," Joe said, walking over to the coffeemaker, scowling when he realized it was still brewing.

"I'm not here early," she said in a harsh whisper. "I never left! We fell asleep last night."

"I guess that explains why your hair's all messy." He propped his hip against the countertop, eyes drifting lower. "And why you're not wearing a bra."

She folded her arms to cover herself. "I couldn't find it."

"I was sleeping on it," Joe said.

That would explain it. "Luckily I woke up before Lily Ann. I would have had a hell of a time explaining why I slept over."

Joe shrugged. "Slumber party?"

She glared at him. Why was he being so blasé about this? "That's not funny. I don't understand why you're not taking this more seriously. She could have seen me *sneaking* from your room at eight in the morning."

"But she didn't. We'll just be more careful next time."

She shook her head. "No. From now on the bedroom is off-limits."

He sighed. "Reily—"

"I mean it, Joe."

"You didn't have fun last night?"

Last night had been…wow. They had lain there wrapped in each other's arms, kissing and touching, making each other feel good. It was almost like being a teenager again, but without the fumbling and awkwardness and the adolescent insecurities. There was no doubt that Joe knew exactly what to do to please a woman. In fact, she never imagined that a man normally so reserved and guarded with his emotions could be so…*passionate.* And they hadn't even made love yet.

Yet. It was inevitable, she knew it. And she *wanted* to. It felt like the next natural step. But it wouldn't happen until they were alone. If that meant renting a room at the Sunrise for a night, so be it. And after last night, that didn't sound like such a bad idea. Of course, that would never happen while his mother was staying there. Plus, the owner was a regular at Joe's Place, which meant that eventually the entire town would hear about it. Not that she cared what anyone thought, but maybe it would be better if they found a place in the next town over or even in Denver. Which would just look as if they had something to hide or were doing something inappropriate.

She sighed to herself.

She knew the logistics could be a little tricky with Lily Ann in the picture, but never imagined it would be *this* complicated.

"So, is that a no?" Joe asked.

She looked up at him. "No?"

"I asked you if you had fun last night."

And she'd been too busy wrestling with her guilty conscience to answer him. "No. I mean, no, it's not a no. It's a yes. I had a lot of fun last night. I just can't help feeling that what we're doing, at least when we do it in your bedroom with Lily Ann in the house, is somehow immoral."

"This really bothers you, doesn't it?"

She nodded.

He shrugged. "Okay, I guess we're back on the couch then."

"You're sure?"

"The last thing I want is for you to be uncomfortable, Reily. We'll figure something out. Maybe Lily Ann can spend the night at a friend's house."

An entire night alone with Joe. The idea gave her a little shiver of excitement. But then Sue came up the stairs, ending the conversation. Reily helped her make breakfast. They all ate together around the kitchen table, and she felt almost as if she was part of the family. For a minute she let herself daydream about what it would be like if they were a real family. Waking every morning in Joe's arms, fixing breakfast and getting Lily Ann ready for kindergarten—which she had excitedly told Reily would start in a month. And maybe even having a baby. A little boy who had Joe's dark hair and deep brown eyes.

But that was all it was, a dream. She had plans, and as much as she might wish that Joe would wait for her, until her career was established and she was ready to settle down, he deserved better than that. He would forget about her. He would find someone who would be everything he needed in a small-town wife and he would marry her and they would live happily ever after. God knows he deserved it after everything he'd been through. She wanted him to be happy, even if that meant being happy with someone other than her.

After breakfast she went home to get ready for work, then Joe hiked her bike into the bed of his truck and they drove to the bar together.

It was a slow day, with very few tips to add to her savings. When Reily's shift ended at four she rode her bike home, thinking that maybe she would give Sue a break and take Lily Ann to the park. She pulled into the driveway, recognizing the car parked across the street and the woman sitting inside.

Chapter Fourteen

Joe's mom sure was persistent, wasn't she?

Ignoring her, Reily parked her bike by the side of the garage and headed up to her apartment to drop her backpack off and change into shorts.

When she heard a knock on the door, she knew exactly who it was.

Joe's mom was dressed in an African-print caftan that seemed to dwarf her already frail appearance, sandals and clunky, wood-bead jewelry.

"Can we talk?" she asked.

Very persistent.

And because Reily felt sorry for her, or maybe because she was a big pushover, she opened the door and let her inside.

"We weren't formally introduced. I'm Veronica."

"I'm Reily," she said, accepting her outstretched hand. It was so small and frail Reily worried that the slightest pressure might splinter the bones.

"The last time I was up here it was used for storage." Veronica gazed around the small room, then back at Reily. "I'm assuming, since you live here and not in the house, that you aren't Joe's wife."

"No, I'm not." His mother looked so tired and pale, Reily gestured to a chair. "Would you like to sit down?"

"Yes, thank you." She dropped into the chair as if her legs simply couldn't hold her another second.

"Are you okay? I mean, no offense, but you don't look so good. Do you need me to call someone for you?"

"I look much worse than I feel. I'm still building my strength back up. The stairs just took a lot out of me."

"Joe mentioned that you were sick."

"Breast cancer," she said. "But we caught it early, so the prognosis is very good. But as you can imagine, going through something like this has a way of making you consider your mortality and think about the mistakes you've made and the wrongs that need righting."

Reily sat in the opposite chair. "Like Joe."

"I don't expect him to forgive me. What I did to him and his dad was unforgivable. But I feel as if he deserves the truth. Which is difficult when he refuses to talk to me."

"Did you expect a heartwarming family reunion?"

"Of course not. But I figured by now he would have come around, if for no other reason than to get rid of me. He's so...*stubborn*."

Reily folded her arms. "I can't imagine who he gets that from."

Veronica smiled sheepishly. "You know, I was only sixteen when I met Joey's dad. My father was a Baptist minister and very strict, and I was going through a rebellious phase, and dating an older man seemed the perfect way to do it."

"How much older?"

"Joe was twenty-nine."

Reily's eyes went wide.

"He didn't know I was so young. I lied and told him I was twenty. By the time he learned the truth, I was already pregnant. You can imagine how upset he was. Of course he did the right thing and asked me to marry him, but I told him no. I wasn't ready to be a wife and mother. I hadn't even graduated high school."

"You weren't married to Joe's dad?"

"No, I was. My parents forced me into it. They said that if I didn't marry him, they would have him brought up on rape charges. I was under the age of consent, so there was no doubt that he would go to prison. I didn't love him and I sure didn't want to be married, but I knew he was a good man and I couldn't bear the thought of ruining his life, so I gave in. I dropped out of school and got married."

"And had Joe."

"When I was seventeen. But it was a disaster right from the start. Joe Senior wanted a wife who would be happy to cook and clean and have his babies. That just wasn't me. I was a terrible cook and a lousy housekeeper and an even worse mother. He and I fought constantly. I knew they would both be better off without me, so I left. I figured he would meet some nice woman, someone who could love them the way I never could. He would marry her and have a couple more kids and they would forget all about me."

It was funny that just that morning Reily had been thinking the same thing about Joe. That it would be so easy for him to replace her. But what if it wasn't? What if, like his dad, Joe never found someone else?

"For the first couple of years I sent birthday cards and

Christmas gifts, but they always came back unopened. I assumed it was because Joe had remarried and started a new family. That's why I never tried to contact Joey. I guess I felt like I didn't have the right after the way I abandoned him."

She looked so sad, so full of regret, Reily couldn't help but feel bad for her. But everyone made choices, and they had to live with them.

"How is it that no one has recognized you? There must be some people in town who knew you."

"I look different than I used to. Besides being much older, I had a bad accident about fifteen years ago. I needed reconstructive surgery."

Karma, Reily wondered, or just dumb luck?

"One of the waitresses at Joe's Place mentioned that Joey is divorced, but I haven't noticed anyone coming around to see his daughter."

Reily knew it wasn't her place to tell Veronica anything about Joe's life, and she had no right to get involved, but maybe it would help her understand how vulnerable he still was.

"Joe's wife left two years ago. They don't see her anymore."

"Oh dear," she said softly. "I had no idea."

"It was pretty rough on him and his daughter."

"You think I should leave him alone."

"It doesn't matter what I think. It's none of my business."

"Maybe coming here was a mistake. Maybe I am too late." She looked so defeated it pulled at Reily's heartstrings. "Maybe he really doesn't care."

She knew she should keep her mouth shut, let Veronica think what she wanted to think, but she just couldn't. "I was watching Joe's daughter last night, so I was here when he came home. He was really upset that you were at the bar."

"So I'm making him miserable, is that what you're saying?"

"All I'm saying is if he really didn't care, it wouldn't have mattered."

Veronica sat a little straighter and the hint of smile crossed her face.

"But, as I said," Reily added with a shrug, "it's really none of my business."

"Well," Veronica said, rising from the chair, appearing stronger than she had been just a few minutes earlier. Looking as though she had a renewed sense of purpose. "I believe I've taken up enough of your time."

Reily stood. "It was nice talking to you."

Veronica smiled. "You too."

"I hope everything works out."

She walked to the storm door and pulled it open, then she turned back around, hand still clutching the handle, and said, "Thank you, Reily."

Then she was gone, leaving Reily to wonder if she'd done the right thing.

"It's Friday," Joe told Steve Richards, the bassist for Thunder Sky, the band that had been headlining at the bar every Saturday night for the last eight months. Until this weekend apparently, because Steve had just cancelled on him. "There's no way I'm going to find another band to replace you guys by tomorrow."

"Dude, I'm really sorry. Jake had a family emergency. His dad had a stroke so he flew back to Pasadena this morning. He's not sure when he'll be back."

What had begun as a pretty good week was swiftly going to hell. His liquor distributor had screwed up his latest order, leaving them short on several brands they needed for the weekend, and after paying through the nose to fix it, the air conditioner was acting up again. To top that off his "mother" had been in last night for dinner, and was back again for lunch today. From where he stood at the bar, Joe glanced her way. She didn't look as pale as she had the other night, and she'd ordered a burger this time instead of her usual salad. Not that it made a difference to him what she ate. She wasn't hounding his employees any longer, but her presence alone was enough to keep him on edge. And the longer she stayed in town, the more likely it was her identity would be discovered, and there was already enough innuendo and conjecture floating around about his and Reily's relationship—which was one of the few things that was actually going right in his life.

But even that could hit the skids when he had to break the news that Mark was coming back next week, and the best Joe could do was maybe squeeze Reily in ten hours a week.

And now he was losing his headlining band. Thunder Sky was responsible for drawing in the majority of his Saturday business. If he couldn't figure something out, he was screwed.

"You can't manage without Jake?" he asked Steve.

"Dude, he's our lead singer."

"No one else sings?"

"Backup, but not lead. So unless you want an instrumental set, or better yet, if you know someone who could sing for him, we're not performing."

"I can sing for him."

Joe and Steve both turned to Reily, who stood behind the bar and had clearly been listening to their conversation while she polished wineglasses—because, despite having had the dishwasher serviced, the stemware continued to come out spotted.

"I know pretty much all the songs you guys play and the ones that I don't, I can learn by tomorrow night. That is, if Joe doesn't mind filling in for me at the bar."

Steve turned to Joe. "Is she joking?"

"She has a great voice," Joe told him. Granted, he had only heard her sing lullabies while perched on the edge of his daughter's bed. How she would do onstage, what kind of performer she would be, he couldn't say. But it couldn't hurt to have her try out.

"I don't know if the other guys would go for it," Steve said.

Reily shrugged. "Whatever. Just thought I would offer."

Joe told Steve, "The least you could do is listen to her sing."

"There's no music," Steve pointed out. "What's she gonna do, sing along to the jukebox?"

"I could sing a cappella," Reily said.

"Right here?" Steve asked.

"How about on the stage?" Reily suggested.

Steve looked surprised. "If you're okay with that."

Reily turned to Lindy, who had been listening in. "Can you handle things without me for a few minutes?"

"Absolutely," Lindy said. "I've been wondering when I was going to hear you sing."

"Joe, you want to turn on the mic?" Reily asked.

Joe crossed the dance floor to the stage to fire up the sound system and kill the jukebox. The sudden absence of music earned him curious looks from everyone having lunch. Reily climbed up behind him and he handed her the mic. If she was nervous at all, it didn't show. Weirdly enough, he was, though he wasn't sure why. She wouldn't be on her way to Nashville to sing professionally if she couldn't handle singing onstage, right?

He hopped down and walked back to the bar where Steve stood, arms folded, looking as though he was expecting an amateur performance.

"Any special requests?" Reily asked, her voice sounding steady and confident through the bar speakers.

"You know anything by Lady A?" Lindy called out.

"That just happens to be one of my favorite bands," Reily said with a grin. "How about 'American Honey'?"

With everyone's attention riveted to the stage, Reily took a deep breath, closed her eyes and started to sing. And Joe stopped breathing.

It was a sweet song about a simple country girl who lost her innocence and wanted to get it back. Maybe he was biased, but in his entire life Joe had never heard a song sung more beautifully, or with more heart. And now he knew, without a shadow of doubt, she was going to make it big. She would be a star. She would leave Paradise and go to Nashville, and there wasn't a damned thing he could or *would* do to stop her. Because the last thing Reily needed was some guy and his kid holding her back. He could never be that selfish again, not after what he had done to Beth.

She finished the song to a roar of applause and catcalls.

"Thank you," she said with her sweet smile, bowing to her audience, then she turned the mic off and jumped down from the stage. Joe felt himself grinning as he looked over at Steve. He was slowly shaking his head, a stunned expression on his face.

Reily walked over to him and said, "So, what did you think?"

"Jesus," Steve said. "Where did you learn to sing like that?"

Reily smiled. "Does that mean I passed the audition?"

"Hell, I'm convinced. Can you come by my place for rehearsal tomorrow afternoon? Two o'clock?"

"I'm supposed to work," Reily said, looking to Joe.

"Go to the rehearsal," he said. "We'll find someone to cover you."

Reily turned to Steve. "I guess I'll be there."

Steve wrote his address down on a napkin that Reily stuffed into the back pocket of her jeans.

After he was gone, Joe asked Reily, "Can I talk to you in my office for a minute?"

She called to Lindy, "I'll be right back," then followed Joe into the back. The second they were inside his office with the door closed, he slid his arms around her, pulled her close and planted a slow, deep kiss on her.

"Hmm, that was nice," she said, smiling up at him. "What was that for?"

"Because you're an amazing woman, Reily Eckardt. I had no idea you could sing like that."

"You've heard me sing to Lily Ann."

"Not like that. That was…" He shook his head, at a loss to adequately express his awe. How could the people of her hometown ever doubt her? "You're going to make it, Reily. You're going to be a star."

She grinned up at him. "I know."

Only now did he realize that all this time, somewhere deep down, he'd let himself believe that Reily wouldn't go. That she would change her mind and decide to stay with him. Or if she did go, she would miss him and Lily Ann so much it wouldn't be long before she came back. Just as he'd felt about his wife. But that wasn't going to happen, he knew that now. And despite that, he wanted

Reily even more, *needed* her, in a way that he'd never needed anyone before. Not even Beth.

All he could do now was make the best of their last few weeks together. And then when the time came, let her go.

Chapter Fifteen

Reily's debut Saturday night as temporary lead singer for Thunder Sky was an enormous hit. Everyone Joe talked to raved about her talent, and by Sunday afternoon the entire town was buzzing. And though Reily had earned the right to bask in the glow of her success, she handled the attention with the utmost grace and humility. Even when Jill, who had been on her very best behavior the past couple days, swallowed her pride and told Reily she had a "really nice voice," and Reily had every right to be smug, she had smiled and thanked her instead.

The Saturday gig was a new source of income for Reily, but after splitting the money with the four other band members, it didn't amount to much. And though Joe had racked his brain, he hadn't come up with a solution to the scheduling situation. He broke it to her during Sunday supper.

"It's okay, Joe," she said with an understanding he

didn't feel he deserved. "Mark has worked for you for a long time. Of course you have to give him his job back."

"But I promised you six weeks," he said.

"Aunt Sue, could I have more chili?" Lily Ann asked, holding out her bowl.

"Sure, sweetheart." Sue stood, taking the bowl, and asked Joe and Reily, "Anyone else want more?"

"No, thanks," Reily said, and Joe shook his head. The truth was that he felt a little sick to his stomach. He was a man of his word, and he hated to let Reily down.

Sue filled Lily Ann's bowl, set it in front of her and sat back down at the kitchen table. They usually ate Sunday supper in the dining room, but the four of them had spent the day at the lake and hadn't gotten back until after seven. They were all exhausted after a day of swimming and sun, so Sue had warmed up the leftover chili and made corn bread from a mix.

"I can probably squeeze you in ten hours a week," Joe said. "And if anyone calls in sick, the shift is yours, no question."

"I'll figure something out," Reily said. "Maybe they could use someone part-time at the diner."

"I feel lousy for doing this to you."

She shrugged. "Worst case, I stay a couple of weeks longer."

God knows he would love for her to stick around, but he couldn't be selfish about this. Besides, the longer she stayed, the harder it would be when she did finally leave.

"You know," Joe said. "I could lend you what you need—"

Reily shook her head. "Absolutely not."

"But I have the money. You can take as long as you want paying me back."

"It's sweet of you to offer, but this is something I need to do on my own."

"I think I may have a solution to the problem," Aunt Sue said.

Joe pushed his bowl away. "I'd love to hear it."

"Ever since my friend Irene moved to Palm Springs she's been nagging me to come visit, but I couldn't just up and leave with no one else to watch Lily Ann. I was thinking, why couldn't Reily take over for a couple of weeks?"

Lily Ann, who he hadn't even realized was paying attention to the conversation, bolted upright in her chair and her eyes lit like firecrackers. "Could she, Daddy? Could Reily babysit me? *Pleeeeeze!*"

As far as Joe could tell, it was the perfect solution. But that didn't mean Reily would want to do it. "What do you think?" he asked her.

"It sounds like a great idea to me," Reily said.

"Yeah!" Lily Ann screeched, getting so excited she flailed her arms and nearly knocked her milk over. Joe managed to grab it a second before it toppled from the table.

Lily Ann bit her lip, smiling sheepishly. "Oops."

"Be careful," Joe warned her, using a napkin to soak up the milk that had splashed over the side. "If Reily sees what a handful you can be she might change her mind."

"I'll be *really* good," Lily Ann told Reily earnestly. "I promise."

"I know you will, sweetheart," Reily said with a smile, chucking her under the chin.

"I'll run home and give Irene a call right now," Sue said, getting up and carrying her bowl to the sink. "I'm sure she'll be thrilled with the idea."

Lily Ann helped clear the table, then went into the living room to watch television while Joe and Reily loaded the dishwasher. By the time they finished and went in to check on her, she was out cold.

"I guess all the swimming wore her out," Reily said.

"I'm going to put her to bed," Joe said, scooping her limp little body up off the couch. "I'll be down in a minute."

He carried Lily Ann upstairs and laid her in bed in her clothes. He pulled the covers up over her and kissed her forehead. For a minute he just stood there, watching her sleep. He hoped this new babysitting arrangement wouldn't be too confusing for Lily Ann. He had explained to her that he and Reily were just friends and that she would be leaving in a few weeks, and Lily Ann seemed to have no trouble grasping that. But he never could be sure what went on in her little head. He hoped she understood that Reily was a babysitter and not a stand-in mother.

When he walked downstairs, Aunt Sue was back.

"It's all settled," she told him. "Irene said to come as soon as I could, so I went online and booked a flight for Tuesday afternoon. That will give me all day tomorrow to pack and make out a schedule for Reily."

"Sounds perfect," Joe said.

"I can't thank you enough for doing this," Reily told her.

"I'm the one who's thankful," Sue said. "Without you I would never be able to take this kind of vacation. Joe's schedule makes it next to impossible to find someone to replace me for any extended amount of time."

Reily's cell phone rang and she pulled it out of her pocket to check the display. "It's Steve. I'd better take this."

When she stepped out onto the front porch, Joe asked Aunt Sue, softly enough so that Reily wouldn't hear, "You haven't ever mentioned to Reily what I pay you, have you?"

She smiled. "Why do I get the feeling she's going to be making considerably more than I do?"

God knows he had tried to pay Sue more, but she insisted on taking the barest minimum. "I plan to pay her enough so that she can leave in six weeks like she planned."

"I would think you'd like to keep her here as long as possible."

"I would only be delaying the inevitable. She has a plan and I have no right to hold her back. I'm not going to make that mistake again."

"Maybe she'll change her mind and decide to stay."

"No, she won't." He knew Aunt Sue liked Reily, *everyone* did, and she wanted Joe to be happy, but it just wasn't meant to be.

"I guess I should get home and start putting that list together for Reily. I'll bring it by in the morning."

"Sounds good."

After she left, Joe sat down on the couch waiting for Reily. She came back inside a few minutes later.

"Well, that was an interesting conversation," she told Joe.

"Is something wrong?"

She sat on the couch beside him and he looped an arm around her shoulders. "Apparently Jake, Thunder Sky's lead singer, is not coming back. The stroke was so bad that his dad has to retire, and he wants Jake to take over the family business. Steve and the other guys want me to take his place permanently."

"What did you tell them?"

"That I'm leaving in a couple weeks, but I'd be happy to fill in until they find someone else. That is, if we can find someone to watch Lily Ann while I'm performing. As long as you're okay with that."

"If you tell them no, I lose my headlining band, so I'm very okay with it. I'm sure we can find someone to watch Lily Ann for a couple of hours Saturday evening."

"You can deduct whatever it costs from what you planned to pay me."

"Okay," he said, even though he would do no such thing. But she would never know that.

"How much are you planning to pay me, by the way?"

"For two full weeks? Minus a couple hours Saturday night?" He pretended to do the math in his head, then quoted her a number. One that was more than double what he paid Aunt Sue.

"Granted, I haven't actually babysat anyone since the late nineties, but that sounds like an awful lot of money."

"Don't forget that you won't just be babysitting. You'll be cooking, too. And cleaning up after Lily Ann."

"It's more than I would have made at the bar, even with tips."

"It's more hours, and in my opinion, harder work. You know what they say about stay-at-home moms, they do the work of something like three full-time jobs." He realized how that sounded and added, "Not that I'm suggesting you're a stand-in mom."

"I knew what you meant."

"My point is, it's a tough job."

"Well, between that and what I'll get performing with Thunder Sky, I'll definitely have enough money to leave on schedule."

"That's good."

She looked up at him. "Is it?"

No, actually. It completely sucked, but he couldn't tell her that. So he settled for, "It's what you want."

Her look said maybe that wasn't the case, that maybe things were beginning to change. Or maybe it was just wishful thinking. As much as he wanted to ask, wanted to know what was going on in her head, he kept his mouth shut. He would not say or do anything to influence her decisions.

There was a soft rap on the front door, so soft he almost didn't hear it. "I wonder who that could be."

"Maybe it's Sue," Reily said.

"Why would Aunt Sue knock?"

"With you and I here alone, do you honestly think she would just walk in?"

He hadn't thought about that. "Good point."

He got up and pulled the door open, expecting it to be Aunt Sue. He mumbled a curse when he found that it was his mother standing there. He was not in the mood to deal with her right now.

"What do you want?" he asked through the screen door.

"Is Lily Ann in bed?"

He frowned. "Why?"

"Because I'm guessing that you don't want her to know who I am. That's why I came by so late."

"Yes, she's in bed, and as I've told you repeatedly, I don't want to talk to you."

"Then you'll be happy to know that I'm leaving."

Leaving? Was that possible? Or was she just using a reverse psychology tactic on him? Did she think that if she convinced him she was really going to go, he would suddenly have a change of heart and agree to talk to her?

He stepped out onto the porch. "Guess you couldn't hold out as long as it takes, huh?"

"I guess not."

She hadn't even made it two weeks. And when the

only thing he should be feeling was relieved, why did he instead feel as if he'd been slighted or cheated?

"I got what I came here for," she said.

"You did?"

"I guess I just needed to see that, despite what I've done to you, you're okay."

He folded his arms. "And now you think I am?"

"You have a beautiful daughter and lots of friends. You run a successful business and people obviously respect you. I would say you're doing pretty well. I guess...I guess I just wanted to know that you're happy."

"You could have saved yourself a lot of time and just asked me."

"Even if you had talked to me, I think I needed to see for myself, and I have. I can also see that my being here is upsetting you, so I'm going to go, and you aren't ever going to see me again. I promise."

Just like that, she was going to leave? She was going to give up without a fight, walk out of his life again, without an explanation as to why it had taken her this damned long to pop back into his life?

And isn't that what he wanted? What he'd been telling her he wanted? Why now did he seem to be having second thoughts? Was he really prepared to let her go and never know what had happened, why she'd abandoned him?

Tears hovered at the edges of her lids, but she blinked them back and squared her shoulders, flashing him a shaky smile. "Goodbye, Joey."

She turned and crossed the porch, then descended the stairs. As her foot hit the concrete walk he heard himself say, "So, you're leaving tonight?"

She stopped and slowly looked back up at him. Though

it was pretty dark, he thought he saw hope in her eyes. "Tomorrow morning."

"What time?"

"Early."

"You'll probably want to stop for breakfast before you go."

She paused, then said, "Probably."

"Well, if you were to be at the diner at, say, nine o'clock, I might see you there."

"Might?" she asked, and there was a quaver in her voice.

"Yeah." It was the best he could do.

"Okay." She turned and walked to her car, which was parked in the street in front of the house.

He opened the front storm door and walked inside. Reily was still sitting on the couch waiting for him. As he sat down beside her she didn't say a word.

"I guess you heard that," he said.

She took his hand, lacing her fingers through his. "Do you want to talk about it?"

"No."

She gave his hand a squeeze. "Okay."

He dropped his head against the back of the couch and sighed. "Am I doing the right thing?"

She shrugged. "Does it feel like the right thing?"

"I don't know. She just looked so…pathetic."

"She looked pretty pathetic the first time she was here, too."

"At first I thought she was just trying to con me into talking to her. But when I realized she was really going…" He shook his head. "I guess that knowing she was leaving, realizing I wouldn't get another chance…"

"She's your mother. There's no shame in wanting to hear what she has to say."

"What if I don't like what she has to say?"

"You might not, but maybe you need to hear it anyway."

She was right, but he refused to analyze it to death. "Let's talk about something else," he said.

"I have an even better idea." She swung her leg over him so that she was straddling his lap. Then she leaned in and kissed him—a sweet kiss, with the promise of so much more—and whispered against his lips, "Let's not talk at all."

Chapter Sixteen

Reily had never really considered herself domestic. She'd always kept her apartment tidy, and would cook the occasional meal, but the duties of, say, a stay-at-home mom, always struck her as pretty monotonous and boring. But this past week, taking care of Lily Ann, she'd had more fun than she'd ever had slinging drinks and filling peanut dishes.

They made cartoon shaped pancakes for breakfast and baked cookies for afternoon treats. They took walks to the park where they would eat picnic lunches on a blanket in the grass, and do silly things like chase butterflies and play in the sandbox and push each other on the swings. And when a supply list came in the mail from Lily Ann's new teacher, Joe lent Reily his truck so she could take Lily Ann school shopping, since kindergarten was only a few weeks away.

But Reily's favorite part of the day was the evening.

She and Lily Ann would shut off the television, cuddle up on the couch together and read books. Then she would get Lily Ann into her jammies and tucked into bed and sing her lullabies until she drifted off to sleep. After that, Reily would curl up on the couch with a book, or turn on a sitcom rerun, waiting excitedly for Joe to come home from work, loving the shiver of anticipation when she saw his headlights flash across the front window as he pulled into the driveway. She loved the smile he gave her when she greeted him at the door and the feel of his body as he pulled her close, the softness of his lips as he kissed her hello. The sense of companionship as they talked about each other's day, the feeling of intimacy when they shared private things about themselves, made her realize that their relationship was as much about friendship as sexual attraction. Not that there was any shortage of that either.

It had been so hard to keep their physical relationship within her moral boundaries. The closer they grew, the more it seemed to her like the next natural step, to solidify their feelings for one another. Unfortunately, with Sue gone, it was harder than ever to find any time alone. But on Sunday, a week and a half before she was scheduled to climb on a bus and leave Paradise—leave Joe and Lily Ann forever—they *finally* caught a break.

Joe and Reily sat on the front porch swing, watching the sunset, exchanging secret smiles and stealing the occasional caress, talking about everything and nothing, while Lily Ann sat on the porch with a coloring book and crayons.

"Did I mention that Veronica emailed me this morning?" Joe said offhandedly, as if the fact that they were communicating, even if it was only electronically, wasn't pretty fantastic.

He almost hadn't gone to the diner that morning to

meet his mother. It had taken him ten minutes of debating before he'd even walked out the door, then another ten of sitting in the driveway in his truck with the motor running before he'd finally left. And he'd admitted later that he'd driven around another fifteen minutes before he'd finally pulled into the diner lot.

And though it had by no means been a touching family reunion, he said the conversation had been very civilized and he'd agreed to keep in touch by email. And that was a start.

"What did she have to say?"

"Just some things about my dad, things I asked her."

Things he clearly wasn't ready to share with Reily, but that was okay.

"How's this one, Reily?" Lily Ann asked, holding up her latest masterpiece. Since she was going to be in real school soon, she had decided that it was imperative she learn to color inside the lines.

"It looks beautiful, sweetheart. I like the purple flowers."

"And the purple trees," Joe said softly. "And the purple grass and the purple animals."

Reily gave him a playful nudge. "She *likes* purple."

"Which is a good thing, considering most of her new school clothes are purple, too."

"Hey, you said to let her pick out what she liked. Encourage her to be her own person. Besides, aren't you the one who bought her the purple bike and the purple sheets and painted her bedroom walls purple?"

He just grinned.

A truck pulled down the street and rolled to a stop in front of the house. Lily Ann shot up as if she were on springs. "Aunt Emily!"

She darted down the porch stairs and met Emily at the curb, launching herself into her aunt's arms.

"Hey, kiddo!" Emily said, giving her a big squeeze. She smiled up at Joe and Reily and called, "Hey there, you two."

"Hi, Em," Joe said.

"Come see my pictures I colored." Lily Ann grabbed her hand, dragging Emily to the porch.

"Would you like a glass of lemonade?" Reily asked her.

"I can't stay more than a minute. My dog Ella is going to have her puppies tonight, and I promised Lily Ann she could help me."

"Yeah!" Lily Ann hopped excitedly. "Can I, Daddy? Can I?"

"Of course you can," Joe said.

"I thought she could stay the night, then I could take her with me to Beau's in the morning. I could have her back here by supper if that works for you."

Which meant that Reily and Joe would have the entire night to themselves.

Alone.

"Um, yeah, that would be fine," Joe said, laying his hand on the swing beside Reily's, his pinky finger barely touching her. Reily's heart picked up speed and her mouth went dry. When Joe looked down at her she knew exactly what he was thinking, because she was thinking the same thing.

"Do I get to see baby Kevin?" Lily Ann asked Emily.

"You sure will. Now, get a move on and pack a bag. I don't want to leave Ella alone for too long."

"Okay!" Lily Ann bolted for the door.

"Don't forget your toothbrush!" Joe called as it banged shut behind her.

Reily asked Emily, "Who is baby Kevin?"

"The nephew of my friend Beau. His half sister passed away a couple of months ago and left her infant son, Kevin, in his care. He's been taking care of him ever since and recently started the process to adopt him."

"How sad," Reily said. "Not that he's adopting him, I mean, but that his mother just died."

"Beau will take good care of him."

"He sounds like a lucky little boy."

Joe casually draped his arm across the back of the swing, letting his fingers barely brush her shoulder and her heart went berserk.

"So, I understand you've been a big hit singing with Thunder Sky," Emily told Reily. "I'd love to see you perform."

"Well, next Saturday is your last chance. After that I'm leaving for Nashville."

Emily looked surprised. "Oh, I didn't realize that you were still going."

A lot of people in town seemed to be laboring under that same misconception. "A week from Wednesday, if all goes as planned."

"Well then, I'll have to be sure to come by the bar this Saturday."

Joe ran a single finger down Reily's nape, and she shivered at his feather-light touch. But he pulled his hand away when the front storm door flew open and Lily Ann rushed out, hauling her Cinderella backpack behind her. "I'm ready!"

"Let me check," Joe said, motioning her over. He unzipped the bag and rifled through its contents. "Toothbrush, PJs, clothes for tomorrow...looks good."

He zipped it back up and handed it to her.

"Kiss!" she said, and Joe gave her a hug and a kiss goodbye. Then she held her arms out to Reily. "Kiss!"

Reily kissed and hugged her, too, then watched with a lump in her throat as Emily buckled her into the truck seat. She'd spent so much time with Lily Ann this past week, she was going to miss her.

"Well, you two have fun tonight," Emily said, winking as she got into the driver's seat of her truck and started the engine. There was obviously no doubt in her mind what Reily and Joe would be doing tonight.

The truck had barely pulled away from the curb when Joe's hand settled on Reily's thigh and began to drift slowly back and forth, gradually moving upward.

"So, we've got the house to ourselves tonight," he said. "Anything special you'd like to do?"

"Well," she said thoughtfully, when inside she was ready to burst. "We could watch a movie. Or play a board game. Or we could just sit and talk."

"We could do that," he said, his fingers slipping inside the leg of her shorts.

She sucked in a shuddering breath. "Or I could strip you naked and kiss every conceivable inch of your body."

He looked down at her and smiled. "Last one inside is a rotten egg."

They were barely through the front door when Reily launched herself at Joe. He fumbled with the lock as she tugged him across the room, toward the couch—which he assumed was just out of habit. But he'd be damned if their first time was going to be on that lumpy thing.

"Upstairs," he said.

She looked up at him through the veil of her lashes, wearing a teasing, seductive smile. "What's the rush?"

For weeks now he'd been exercising the utmost control, respecting her wishes, but now he was at the absolute end of his patience. Tonight he was the one in charge, which meant they were having sex—*lots and lots of sex*—and they were doing this his way.

He grabbed hold of her and hiked her up over his shoulder.

"Joe!" she half screeched, half laughed. "What are you *doing?*"

"Taking you to my bedroom. No more couch. In fact, I might just take it out back and *burn* it."

She laughed. "I can walk, you know."

"I'm calling the shots tonight."

"By acting like a caveman?" she said, sounding indignant. "And who says I'm *letting* you call the shots?"

He shouldered his way through the door, walked to the bed and dumped her down in the middle of it. "I do."

"Well, lots of luck with that," she said, and just to assert her authority—at least, that's what he assumed she was doing—she grabbed the hem of her top and pulled it up over her head. Then she unfastened her bra and pulled that off too, pinning him with a *so there* look. He might have been annoyed, but she was damned pretty, and he got distracted looking at her instead. He'd never been the kind of man who favored one part or another on a woman's body. He liked the entire package, and Reily, she was just perfect. Although to be fair, he wasn't getting the complete picture.…

Reily must have read his mind because she reached down, unfastened her shorts and shoved them off. With only her panties left, she was as close to naked as he'd ever seen her. But not naked enough.

He pulled his shirt off, then knelt on the bed beside her. When he touched her belly, just below her navel, she sucked in a quiet breath and her eyes darkened to the color of midnight. With the very tips of his fingers he traced a path along the waist of her panties. "I think these need to go."

"I think they do, too."

He slid them down her legs, and...*oh yeah,* she was definitely the full package.

"Now you," she said. Demanded really.

His brows rose. "Is that an order?"

"As a matter of fact, it is. And do it...sexfully."

His brows rose. *"Sexfully?"*

"You know, like a striptease," she said, pushing herself up on her elbows as if she were settling in to watch.

He was pretty sure she was kidding, but just in case she wasn't, he said, "I'm not exactly the striptease type."

Although, at that moment he was so hot for her, he may have actually done it. But her exaggerated sigh and wry smile told him she was definitely teasing. He took his shorts and boxers off—as unsexfully as always—and the hungry look she gave him, the way her eyes took in every inch of his body, said she didn't need a striptease to get her motor running.

She grinned and summoned him with a crooked finger. "Get over here."

Technically he was supposed to be calling the shots, but this time, he would make an exception.

He crawled up over her, feeling a bit like a tiger stalking its prey. If he had his way, he did intend to ravage her.

Reily opened her arms to him, wrapped them around his shoulders, pulled him against her. And all he could think was *perfect.* They were a perfect fit.

"You know what I just realized?" Reily said.

"What?"

"We're finally alone."

"I know."

"And naked."

They certainly were. "Yep."

"Together," she added, as if there had been any question.

"And it's about damned time," he said.

"So why aren't you kissing me?"

He smiled. "I was just getting to that."

Though he had kissed Reily on a pretty regular basis lately—on the couch, in his truck, in the storage room at the bar and even once in the walk-in freezer—there was just no comparison to doing it naked. He felt almost as if he were kissing her again for the first time. It was exciting and erotic, and it just plain old felt good. But there was something else, too. Something he couldn't quite put his finger on. Something almost...*comforting.* Which seemed like a pretty weird feeling to have when making love to a woman for the first time, and one that he couldn't remember ever having before.

But he liked it.

He wanted to capture it and hold on to it, make it last all night. He tried to take things slow, but Reily, with her moaning and her grinding and her hands that kept finding new places to touch and explore, was making it really difficult to hold *anything* back.

"Please tell me you have a condom," she said breathlessly.

Did she really think he wouldn't have planned ahead for this? He reached over and pulled the drawer on the bedside table open and grabbed the box. She snatched it away from him.

"Let me do it."

"We don't have to rush this," he said.

"It's been over a month, Joe," she said, taking a condom out and tossing the box aside. "I would hardly call that rushing it. Especially if you consider the fact that I've wanted to do this since the first day I met you."

"You have?"

"Yeah, when I wasn't cursing you for being such a big jerk." She ripped the package open with her teeth. "Now, sit up so I can put this on you."

Even though he was supposedly the one calling the shots, he let her suit him up. And when she leaned back and pulled him on top of her, and he sank deep inside of her, out of the blue it hit him, that feeling of comfort that had seemed so strange. It was love.

He *loved* her.

He actually felt a little stupid for not realizing it sooner, and he considered it pretty darned amazing, because he'd honestly questioned whether he even had it in him to love a woman that way again. And at the same time it totally sucked because she was leaving. And even if she felt anything even remotely close to love for him, she wouldn't be around long enough for that love to grow to something worth holding on to.

But they had right now, and when Reily moaned his name and shuddered in his arms as she found her release, he found his too. And later, after making love again, and then a third time, when they lay in each other's arms and her breathing was deep and even and he was sure she was asleep, he told her that he loved her.

For the first and possibly the last time.

Chapter Seventeen

Reily stood in the living room of her tiny apartment, the duffel bag she'd picked up at the secondhand store stuffed with her belongings, her guitar tucked safely into the secondhand case the guys of Thunder Sky had given her during her going-away party last night at the bar. For six weeks this had been home, and it was hard to imagine that she would never see it again.

Leaving this town, and all the wonderful friends she had made, would be the hardest thing she'd ever had to do. For all the years she had lived in Montana, leaving hadn't really been that difficult. Since she lost her parents, she'd always felt a little bit like a visitor in her own life, as if home was a place, a concept, that eluded her. Stuck in the corner of her aunt's apartment or slotted as the "surrogate" daughter, who would never and could never be as special as the "real" one. She'd never felt as if she truly belonged anywhere. Not until she'd met Joe and Sue and Lindy and Lily Ann, and all of her other friends in Paradise. For the first time in a long time, she finally began to feel as if she were home. And now she had to leave that. For a new home, because she was going to make it big, she was going to be a star. Isn't that what she'd spent the last sixteen years convincing every person she knew? She couldn't back down now.

"Need some help?"

Reily turned to find Joe standing in the doorway. She hadn't even heard him come up the stairs. "I just have the one bag."

"We're going to have to leave soon or you'll miss your bus."

It was true that she'd been procrastinating all afternoon. She wanted to savor every last minute she had left here.

She took a deep breath, squaring her shoulders. "Well then, we'd better go."

Sue, Lily Ann and Lindy were waiting for them next to the 'Cuda, which Joe had taken out special for the occasion. "It's where we had our first kiss, so it only makes sense that we have our last one there, too," he'd reasoned, which of course had only made her feel terrible. The idea that she would never kiss Joe again, never feel his arms around her, made her heart sting.

She was surprised to see Lindy there since they had already said goodbye last night. It seemed as though most of the town had shown up. When she left Montana she'd had a grand total of fifteen people at the party Abe threw for her, and probably half of them had only come for the free beer and hot wings.

As Reily approached her, Lindy stepped forward and threw her arms around her. "I am going to miss you so much, Reily. Make sure you email me and tell me how you're doing, and don't forget about us little people when you're playing to sold-out stadiums." She held Reily at arm's length and grinned. "I expect free tickets, and they'd better be front row."

"Absolutely." She turned to Joe's aunt, who had big fat tears running down her cheeks. "Sue…"

"Oh, don't mind me," she said, giving Reily a firm squeeze. "Goodbyes always make me cry. Just promise you'll keep in touch and visit if you can."

"I will," she said, but it was a lie. Once she left here, she knew she could never come back. It would be too hard, too painful. Especially if Joe was seeing someone new. Not that she didn't want him to be happy. She did. But selfish as it was, she wanted the person he was happy with to be her. Which would be tough if they lived over a thousand miles away from each other.

Reily turned to Lily Ann, who was standing off to the side, eyes on the ground, lips stuck out in a pout, kicking at the concrete with the toe of her purple tennis shoe. The shoes they had picked out together.

"Goodbye, Lily Ann."

Lily Ann folded her arms stubbornly. When Reily crouched down to her level, she turned away.

"Lily Ann," Joe scolded. "Say goodbye to Reily."

Lily Ann shook her head, her blond curls swinging.

"That's okay," Reily said. It broke her heart, but she understood. She wanted Reily to stay, and in her young mind, not saying goodbye meant Reily wouldn't really go. She'd felt the same way at her parents' funeral; when everyone was ready to leave the graveside and her aunt told her to say goodbye, she'd refused because it meant that she would never see them again. She'd believed that by refusing to say the words out loud, to even think them, her parents might magically return. Of course they hadn't, and goodbyes had never gotten much easier for her.

"We better go," Joe said. He put her things in the trunk and opened the door for her. She slid into the front seat and buckled her seat belt, barely able to contain the tears stinging her eyes as he started the engine. She looked straight ahead as he pulled out of the driveway.

"She'll be okay," Joe said.

"I just hate that I'm hurting her."

He reached out, covered her hand with his own and laced his fingers through hers. "I know."

"She knew I was leaving. We even kept a calendar counting down the days. We made it into a game. I thought she would be more prepared."

He squeezed her hand. "She was. But *knowing* that a person is leaving doesn't make it any easier when they actually go."

He said that like he was speaking from experience. He'd been putting on a good face all day. All week. But she could tell that he was hurting, even if he was too proud to admit it.

"This is so unfair," she said.

"What is?"

"That I have to choose. You and Lily Ann or my singing career."

"You've worked too hard to quit now."

"Maybe…maybe I don't have to. I could split my time. People do it *all* the time. What if I stayed in Nashville during the week, then flew back here on the weekends? Or spent three weeks there and one week here?"

Joe sighed, not taking his eyes off the road. "I can't do this halfway, Reily. Lily Ann needs someone stable, someone who has time for her. And so do I. I just can't put us in a position where we're second place again. I won't do that to her, and I won't do it to myself."

But you love me, right? He'd said the words that first night they made love. He had thought she was asleep, and she had pretended to be, so she wouldn't have to say what she was feeling in her heart, what she had been feeling almost since the day she met him. That she loved him, too. What would it have accomplished when he knew that she was leaving? Now she wondered if that had been a mistake. Because she felt that, if he would only say the words, if he would just ask her to stay, just one time, she would. And she would be happy, and never regret it, not for a single minute.

Or would she?

Would she begin to feel cheated and unfulfilled? Would she grow to resent Joe and Lily Ann, until it eventually became too painful to stay? Would she hurt them the way Beth had? And was that a risk she could take?

If only she could see the future. If she could predict what she would be feeling a year from now or five years or ten.

Joe headed down Main Street in the direction of Blue Hills, the next city over, where she would catch the bus. It was only a fifteen-minute drive and the closer they got, the harder it was to breathe, as though some invisible force was compressing her lungs and not enough air was getting through. Her hands started to shake and her knees felt funny.

She realized she was having a panic attack. She was off to start her new life and instead of being excited, she was hyperventilating and sweating bullets.

Relax. Slow, shallow breaths.

She kept that up until they pulled into town. The bus was already there, loading passengers. Joe parked in a spot a few yards away.

He was about to get out when she blurted, "Joe, do you want me to stay?"

The blunt question seemed to surprise him, and for several seconds he just sat there, looking conflicted. Then he said, "What difference does it make what I want?"

It made one hell of a difference to her. "Let's put it this way. If I were to say, 'Joe, I've changed my mind and I don't want to go to Nashville anymore,' then you would say…?"

"It doesn't matter what I'd say, because you haven't changed your mind. You're leaving."

He made her want to bang her head against the nearest wall. "Just tell me, do you love me or don't you?"

He closed his eyes, let his head fall back against the seat. "I can't. I can't tell you that."

"Can't, or won't?"

"We better get your things." He got out of the car and walked around to open the trunk. He pulled out her guitar, which he handed to her, then hiked her duffel up over his shoulder. They walked to the bus, where the driver was stowing the luggage away underneath. He set Reily's bag down for him to take.

"Well," he said, turning to Reily. "I guess this is good-bye."

But did it have to be? Because suddenly her heart was racing and her palms were sweating, and right now the idea of actually getting on the bus terrified her far more than the possibility of what might happen if she didn't.

It was probably just nerves, she told herself. Who wouldn't be a little edgy moving to a strange city where they didn't know a living soul? Or have a job or a place to live? Of course she was nervous. Staying here, that didn't make her nervous at all. But if she went to Nashville and failed, the only one to get hurt would be her. Then again, if she stayed here, and that turned out to be the wrong thing, there was so much more at stake. A little girl with a fragile heart and a good man who didn't deserve to be hurt again. Who deserved better than maybes.

"Have a safe trip," Joe said, his jaw tense. "Don't forget to write."

She put her hand on his arm. "I love you, Joe."

He pressed one last hard kiss to her lips. "Goodbye, Reily."

He walked back to his car and she boarded the bus. She found an empty seat somewhere near the middle. She heard Joe's car start and the rumble of the engine as he hit the gas, but no matter how much she wanted to, no matter how she tried, she couldn't make herself look as he drove away.

Sometime in the three days since Reily left, Lily Ann had made up her mind that Reily was coming back, and no matter what he said, no matter how many times he told her it wasn't true, Lily Ann would not be swayed. As if Reily's leaving wasn't hard enough, as if he didn't feel like someone had ripped his heart out of his chest and stomped it with lead boots, he had to constantly remind his daughter that despite what she believed, Reily was not returning.

"She's going to walk me to kindergarten," she told Joe when he tucked her into bed Saturday night. Feeling she probably needed the extra attention, he'd been stopping home to tuck her in every night, but it didn't seem to be doing much good.

"Honey, we talked about this. Aunt Sue will be walking you to school."

"And she'll bring her guitar to my school and play for show-and-tell," she went on as if he hadn't even spoken. "And I'll have the prettiest, bestest singing mommy in the whole kindergarten. Probably the whole *school*."

Now Reily was her mommy? "Lily, baby, Reily is in Nashville, far, far away from here. *Your* mommy is in California."

"Beth is my old mommy," she said, and he was a little taken aback to hear her refer to Beth by her first name. She'd never done that before.

"Reily will be my new mommy," she said, as if she had no doubt whatsoever. Then her expression turned thoughtful. "Dakota's mommy is having a baby and she's gonna have a brother. If Reily had a baby, do you think she would have a boy, too? Because I think I'd rather have a sister."

Either she knew something Joe didn't, or she was completely losing touch with reality. "I think you should stop worrying about it and go to sleep."

"Okay, Daddy. 'Night."

She snuggled down into the pillow and Joe pulled the covers over her. "You want me to read you a story?"

She shook her head. "No, thanks."

"You sure? I came home from work just so I could."

"No, thank you."

"Okay. Pleasant dreams." He kissed her forehead, then got up and walked to the door. As he was closing it behind him, he heard her sing a soft, slightly off-key rendition of one of Reily's lullabies, and a lump the size of the entire state of Colorado lodged in his throat as he headed down the stairs.

"I'm worried about her," he told Sue, who was stretched out on the sofa watching one of her reality shows. "She's got herself convinced that Reily is coming back, and nothing I say can change her mind."

"Maybe she knows something you don't."

"Aunt Sue—"

"It's obvious Reily loves you and you love her. Did you really think Lily Ann wouldn't pick up on that? And you never know, Reily could be sitting in Nashville right now, lonely and miserable, deciding that she wants to come home."

"But this isn't even home. Home is Montana."

"Home is where there's people who love you and you have friends, and Reily has both those things here."

For God's sake, she was just as bad as Lily Ann.

"Reily is not coming back, and everyone is going to be a lot better off when they just accept that."

Aunt Sue shrugged and said, "You're probably right."

Now he had the feeling she was just humoring him.

"I have to get back to work."

"Okay. I'll see you around two-thirty," she said, turning back to her show.

He walked out to his truck and climbed in. Didn't Aunt Sue understand that until they stopped talking like Reily was on some temporary leave of absence, it was impossible for him to put this to rest, to stop having *hope?* Not a minute passed when she didn't cross his mind, when he didn't miss her with his whole heart. Though he had the feeling she'd taken a pretty good-sized chunk of it with her when she'd left.

This is going to get easier, he told himself as he drove

back to the bar, not knowing for sure if he believed his own spiel.

When he got back to work he checked in with Lindy, who assured him that things were running smoothly. The opening band was playing, then Thunder Sky would take the stage. At first he'd thought they might not make it, since they hadn't found a new singer to replace Reily. But then Steve had called yesterday afternoon to say that they would be able to play after all. Joe was relieved, because the last thing he felt like doing right now was interviewing bands. But the idea of hearing them play and listening to the songs that Reily had managed to make her own in the span of a couple weeks actually made him sick to his stomach. So he barricaded himself in his office instead, and though he tried to work, he found the best he could do was stare blindly at his computer screen. Maybe if he looked hard enough, it might give him the answers he was seeking, like how to make this stop hurting so much.

It had hurt when Beth left, too, but that pain had been more for his daughter. In a way, after so many rocky years, Joe had been relieved that it was finally settled, that he could stop tiptoeing around her. But this—what he was feeling now for Reily—it was excruciating.

A while later, when he still had gotten absolutely nothing done, Lindy knocked on his office door and poked her head in. "Joe, we need you out here."

"Need me? Is there a problem?"

"Nope, no problem."

"Then leave me alone," he said, knowing that he sounded like a crab, but not caring.

"Your presence is requested in the bar."

"By *whom?*"

She blew out an exasperated breath. "Would you just come out here. *Please?*"

He didn't want to talk to anyone, including her. But he could see that she wasn't going to leave him alone. "Fine," he said, shoving his chair back from his desk so hard it banged the wall behind him.

He followed her out to the bar, looking around to locate the individual "requesting his presence," and was overcome by an eerie sensation when he realized that *everyone* at the bar was looking at him. Everyone in the dining room as well. He also noticed that there was no music playing. He turned toward the stage, only to discover that everyone on the dance floor was staring at him, too. What the hell was going on? Had he just stepped into a freaking *Twilight Zone* episode?

"Good evening, ladies and gentlemen," someone said over the sound system, and Joe realized that Thunder Sky was onstage and Steve was introducing the band. Four of them, anyway. He didn't see the new singer. Is that why Lindy had called him out here?

"We're going to start the evening with a special request. This song goes out to Joe Miller."

They started to play a song, one he was sure he'd never heard them play before, but there was something vaguely familiar about it. He turned back to Lindy, to ask her what the hell was going on, why they would dedicate a song to him, then froze when he heard a voice begin to sing.

Reily's voice.

No, it wasn't her. It had to be a recording, from some previous performance. This could be some sort of twisted joke they were playing on him, but why would they do that? Then it hit him…she was singing that song, the one she'd sung a cappella for Steve. About the country girl who lost herself and was trying to find a way back home. Back to who she used to be.

He slowly turned, heart pounding, and there she was. He was afraid that he wanted it so badly his mind had summoned the vision of her, or it was a trick of the light, a mirage. But then she looked right at him, smiled at him, and he knew it really was her. Suddenly the stage seemed to be getting closer and he realized that his feet were moving, carrying him toward her, and as he crossed the dance floor the crowd parted like the Red Sea. When he reached the stage he just stood there, gazing up at her while Reily sang to him, and when the song ended and the band launched into the Allman Brothers hit "Jessica"—one that he noted had no vocals—Reily held out her hand and he helped her down.

"What are you doing here?" he shouted over the music.

"I couldn't do it, Joe. I couldn't stay in Nashville. I knew the minute I stepped on that bus that it was a mistake. I made myself sit there for two days, thinking that when I got there I would feel differently, but I only felt worse."

People were watching them, but he didn't care. It was so loud no one more than a foot away would be able to hear them. "How did you get back here?"

"I stepped off the bus, took a cab to the airport and booked the first flight back to Colorado. I called Steve and he picked me up at the airport in Denver."

"Why?"

"Why did I call Steve?"

"No, why are you here? Why did you come back?"

"Because you love me. I know you couldn't tell me at the bus station because you didn't want to influence my decision. You didn't want to do the same thing to me that you did to Beth. You wanted me to make the choice on my own. And I choose to stay here, with you."

He wanted to pull her into his arms and hold her but he couldn't; he was afraid to let himself believe that this could be real. "I do love you, Reily, but I can't ask you to make that sort of sacrifice."

"But you're not. And besides, it's not a sacrifice. Not anymore."

"If you don't go to Nashville and at least try, you're going to regret it the rest of your life. I just can't do that to you."

She grabbed two fistfuls of his shirt and shouted, "Listen to me, Joe. Ever since I lost my parents, there's been this empty place deep inside of me and I filled that with music. It was the only thing that made me feel close to my parents, made me feel whole again. But then I met you and Lily Ann, this whole town, and suddenly that empty space started to fill up again, until it was so full from your love and friendship that it was overflowing. Walking away from that was the hardest thing I've ever done, and the hole it left inside of me…" She shook her head, her eyes welling with tears. "There's no song, no recording contract, no *career* that could ever make me feel as complete, as whole as I feel with you. You're what I want now, Joe. You and Lily Ann."

"But what about singing? You're just going to give it up?"

"Heck, no! You're looking at the new permanent lead singer for Thunder Sky. Music will always be important to me, but my family, they'll always come first."

He believed her. He would be an idiot not to. And when he pulled her into his arms, kissed her hard, the sound of cheers broke out all around them. Maybe he should have been embarrassed, but he was too happy to care. He didn't care who saw them and who gossiped about them tomorrow. He just laughed and Reily did, too.

"Come with me," he said, leading her to the back so he could welcome her back properly, without most of Paradise watching them.

"I love you, Joe," she said when they were in the privacy of his office. "I want us to be a family."

"I love you, too, and we'll definitely be a family," he said. "Just as soon as I can get a ring on your finger."

She grinned up at him, her cheeks flushed, her smile bright. "That sounded a little like a marriage proposal."

"Consider it a sneak peek of what's to come when I actually get the ring."

"How is Lily Ann? I hope she's not too upset."

"Lily Ann is fine. Since the day you left it's as if she already knew you were coming back."

"What do you mean?"

"She's been going on about how you're going to walk her to school and come to her class for show-and-tell. She was even asking whether your baby will be a boy or a girl, because her personal preference is a little sister."

She reached up, cupping his cheek. "A little girl would be nice. Or a boy. Or maybe even one of each. If that's something you want."

"Oh, I definitely want it." He wanted to spend the rest of his life making her happy, because being with her was the only thing that could make him happy, too.

"I have an idea," he said. "Why don't we go to the house so Lily Ann can see that you're back?"

"Are you sure you want to wake her?"

"I'm sure. She's going to be really happy to see you."

"The feeling is mutual."

He cradled her face in his hands and kissed her softly, unable to believe his luck. He'd let her go and she'd come back to him. "What will you tell your friends back in Montana when they learn you never made it big in Nashville? That you settled for a life in Paradise, Colorado?"

She gave him that sweet smile and rose up on her toes to press a kiss to his lips. "Well, first off, I'll be sure they know that I didn't settle one bit. And then I'll tell them that I gave up my Nashville dream to be with the *man* of my dreams instead."

* * * * *

#2197 THE LAST SINGLE MAVERICK
Montana Mavericks: Back in the Saddle
Christine Rimmer
Steadfastly single cowboy Jason Traub asks Jocelyn Bennings to accompany him to his family reunion to avoid any blind dates his family has planned for him. Little does he know that she's a runaway bride—and that he's about to lose his heart to her!

#2198 THE PRINCESS AND THE OUTLAW
Royal Babies
Leanne Banks
Princess Pippa Devereaux has never defied her family except when it comes to Nic Lafitte. But their feuding families won't be enough to keep these star-crossed lovers apart.

#2199 HIS TEXAS BABY
Men of the West
Stella Bagwell
The relationship of rival horse breeders Kitty Cartwright and Liam Donovan takes a whole new turn when an unplanned pregnancy leads to an unplanned romance.

#2200 A MARRIAGE WORTH FIGHTING FOR
McKinley Medics
Lilian Darcy
The last thing Alicia McKinley expects when she leaves her husband, MJ, is for him to put up a fight for their marriage. What surprises her even more is that she starts falling back in love with him.

#2201 THE CEO'S UNEXPECTED PROPOSAL
Reunion Brides
Karen Rose Smith
High school crushes Dawson Barrett and Mikala Conti are reunited when Dawson asks her to help his traumatized son recover from an accident. When sparks fly and a baby on the way complicates things even more, can this couple make it work?

#2202 LITTLE MATCHMAKERS
Jennifer Greene
Being a single parent is hard, but Garnet Cottrell and Tucker MacKinnon have come up with a "kid-swapping" plan to help give their boys a more well-rounded upbringing. But unbeknownst to their parents the boys have a matchmaking plan of their own.

REQUEST YOUR FREE BOOKS!
2 FREE NOVELS PLUS 2 FREE GIFTS!

❧ Harlequin®

SPECIAL EDITION
Life, Love & Family

*Harlequin® American Romance® presents a
brand-new miniseries* HARTS OF THE RODEO.

*Enjoy a sneak peek at AIDAN: LOYAL COWBOY
from favorite author Cathy McDavid.*

Ace walked unscathed to the gate and sighed quietly. On
the other side he paused to look at Midnight.

The horse bobbed his head.

Yeah, I agree. Ace grinned to himself, feeling as if he,
too, had passed a test. *You're coming home to Thunder
Ranch with me.*

Scanning the nearby vicinity, he searched out his mother.
She wasn't standing where he'd left her. He spotted her
several feet away, conversing with his uncle Joshua and
cousin Duke who'd accompanied Ace and his mother to the
sale.

He'd barely started toward them when Flynn McKinley
crossed his path.

A jolt of alarm brought him to a grinding halt. She'd
come to the auction after all!

What now?

"Hi." He tried to move and couldn't. The soft ground
pulled at him, sucking his boots down into the muck. He
was trapped.

Served him right.

She stared at him in silence, tendrils of corn-silk-yellow
hair peeking out from under her cowboy hat.

Memories surfaced. Ace had sifted his hands through
that hair and watched, mesmerized, as the soft strands
coiled around his fingers like spun gold.

Then, not two hours later, he'd abruptly left her bedside,
hurting her with his transparent excuses.

She stared at him now with the same pained expression she'd worn that morning.

"Flynn, I'm sorry," he offered lamely.

"For what exactly?" She crossed her arms in front of her, glaring at him through slitted blue eyes. "Slinking out of my room before my father discovered you'd spent the night or acting like it never happened?"

What exactly is Ace sorry for? Find out in
AIDAN: LOYAL COWBOY.

Available this July wherever books are sold.